The Paris Plot

Tammy Juola

PublishAmerica
Baltimore

First printing

ISBN: 1-4137-2946-0
PUBLISHED BY PUBLISHAMERICA, LLLP
www.publishamerica.com
Baltimore

Printed in the United States of America

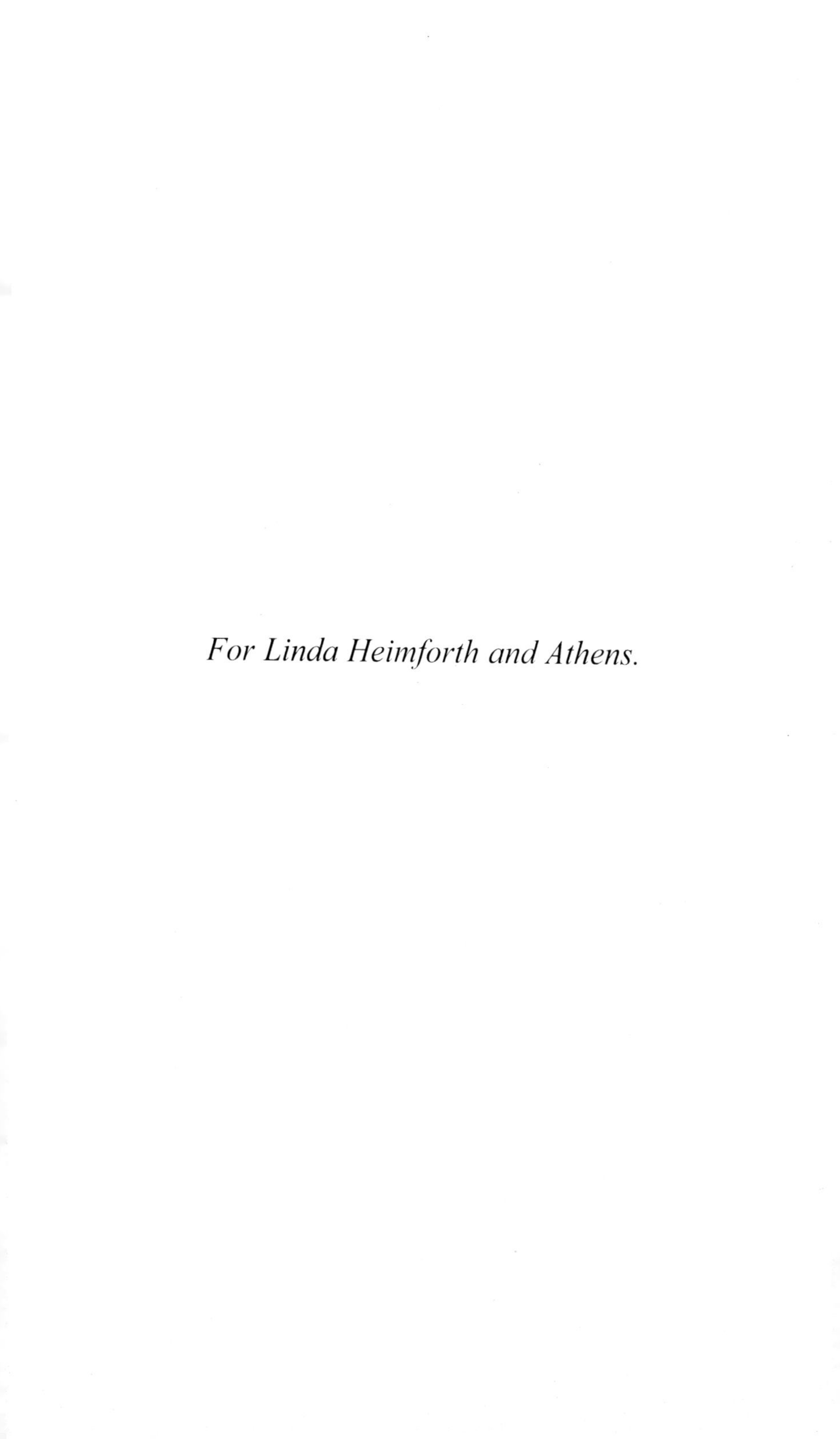

For Linda Heimforth and Athens.

The people, places, and particulars of *The Paris Plot* are pretty much products of the author's imagination. Any resemblance to Parisians, Germans, Americans, or aliens not yet present and accounted for is supposed to be some kind of coincidence.

Prologue

Parc Chien, Paris
Sunset, 20 February

As fireworks exploded across the Eiffel Tower, a huddle of lawn bowlers gazed up at the Parisian pyrotechnics. Meanwhile, Danielle Seabright used the opportunity to snatch one of their *boules* balls from the perimeter of their sandy court. Unaccustomed to committing horrid crimes, she nevertheless found it mildly amusing to take things that didn't belong to her. She had no need to pocket an overgrown marble, but she no longer regarded such indulgences as sins. According to her newly psychologized worldview, she found she could blame just about anything on just about anyone other than herself.

Dressed in an Inverness cape and clogs, Seabright drew mocking stares from the snobbish Right Bank *boulevardiers* who dubbed her Little Red Riding Hood, but she fit in better at the literary cafes of the Left Bank where Academic Broke passed for Artistic Bohemian. Her bottle green eyes and flowing black hair attracted the attention of a man who derived pleasure from exploiting others' pain. The unnatural stalker listed her cavalier pilfering in the catalog of his mind, knowing any unconfessed sin was his ticket in.

CHAPTER ONE

The Eiffel Tower, Paris
Sunset, 20 February

"What are we going to do with the body?" asked a glib Hawk Devlin. Migratory, lupine, handsome as a fallen angel, deeply disturbed yet undisturbable, the Parisian predator swaggered with his wool coat cracked open as if both revealing and concealing something. Hawk's noodly, short-cropped hair looked as if it belonged on a Roman emperor: Caligula.

The stalker's unsuspecting new companion, James Woodlawn Seabright, shifted uncomfortably inside his Civitas Dei varsity jacket. Realizing he couldn't outsmart the killer, he hoped he could at least outrun him. "What are *you* going to do with the body? You're the one who killed him. I was a history major, so the only dead bodies I've ever seen were in books."

Hawk stepped over the victim as if he were mere roadkill. "Then do come to the Louvre with me where you'll enjoy a cornucopia of corpses elegantly displayed in living color on dead museum walls." His eyes strolled up the Eiffel Tower's metallic webbing that towered over him like a Hong Kong skyscraper. Still, he felt as if he were in complete control of it. "James, what I see is a rather lovely little ledge up there and a dreadfully dead body down here..."

"You aren't going to make it look like a suicide," James protested.

"It looks like a murder now. We can do better than that."

"It looks like a murder because it was a murder." The cowardly jock tugged his white turtleneck over his chin to conceal his face, and his fear.

Hawk cranked his head mechanically as if he were a robot that could hear colors and see sounds. His detached demeanor was making him even more unpredictable than James could ever have imagined. "I suggest you keep your opinions to yourself if you enjoy having a pulse."

The American athlete made fists out of his quivering fingers. "Threaten me and I'll turn you in to the Paris police."

"Turn me in and you turn yourself in. Yours are the fingerprints on that *boules* ball."

James could not believe his ears. "Is that why you insisted on taking so many pictures of me with the victim before he became your victim?"

"Like I said on the Metro, anyone who trusts me gets burned," Hawk bragged.

The college boy knew he was about to get a real education, even though he had come to Europe for athletics, not academics. "Why are you doing this to me?"

"Because you let me."

With eyes closed, James raked his scalp until his fingernails filled with dead skin. He did not know Paris well enough to escape Hawk's plot, let alone his own stupidity. "What have you been carrying around in that bag all day?"

"A scalpel and a lovely set of kitchen knives. I'm traveling light this trip."

"Law school rejected you, so now you're doing everything possible to be wanted by the law? That's perverse. I don't doubt your wrist isn't even infected. I bet you wore that surgical glove so you wouldn't leave any fingerprints."

Hawk rolled back his glove to expose a slice of bleeding flesh. "I hope you're satisfied. Now help me roll the body on its side so we can tuck a suicide note in the jacket."

The track and field star felt too weak to roll anything. "Funky fiddlesticks. I'm not thinking straight after that stupid champagne and chateaux tour, but I bet your plan has more holes in it than a golf course."

Hawk seized James' arm as if it were the lever on a slot machine. "The *gendarmes* will swarm us like flies on feces when they realize we're communicating with a corpse without the proverbial card table and crystal ball, so do as I say."

James rotated the victim's torso, though he felt like putting his hands to better use by wringing Hawk's neck. "Did you have to waste him beneath the world's most famous landmark? Why didn't you dive into the sewers of Paris to do your dirty deed?"

"Dirt is an illusion; it owns no reality but the reality you give it. An opportunity to ice him presented itself when he disgorged his digestibles. I don't waste the opportunities God gives me."

"No, you waste the people God gives you. You're as twisted as the rope God will hang you on. My golden opportunity to score gold at the Olympics may now be gone with the wind, thanks to this bout of backsliding. The further I stray off course, the more I wish I had kept to the straight and narrow." James shook his head disconsolately. "I'm glad I didn't see you do it."

"Me too. Now you can't testify against me." Hawk glared at him, effectively buying his silence. "If he hadn't shown off his shekels, he might be alive to do the can-can at another cabaret tonight. He should've realized a poor student would kill for his stash of cash."

"You aren't poor, and you weren't exactly a poor student in our French class, either."

"Engage your auditory orifices, James. I didn't say *I* was a poor student. I am a student, however, of others' stupidity. I seduced one stupid soul into a season of sexual experimentation by convincing him that infidelity has its positive side. I told him Henry IV had 53 mistresses, yet he was quite able to end the religious wars in France. He fell for that ill-logic, why? Because he wanted to. Tempt people with the right rope and they'll hang themselves every time."

"You would've made a good lawyer—a bad person but a good lawyer."

Spite sizzled in Hawk's eyes as a spasm of rage crossed his face like a current of negative energy waiting to unleash itself. "You're on to me. Now I shall have to kill you."

"That isn't funny."

"It wasn't meant to be." A well-polished wingtip kicked sand on to James' shy loafers. "He didn't know me, so the bobbies won't be able to link this spot of unpleasantness to me."

"Bobbies? You're confusing your countries, your royal heinous."

"No. We cosmopolitan types just opt for more colorful language than you Yanks."

"Colorful language seems to concern you more than the color of this corpse."

"All color exists sommmewherrrrre under the rainbow, does it not?" Hawk began humming his obnoxious rendition of a *Wizard of Oz* tune. "We have ourselves a predicament, my pretty, but I am the king of the forest, I am, I am, I am that I am."

"You are too weird for words." James dusted the sand off his chinos to buy time while calculating whether he could make it to a *bateau mouche* before the cops engulfed the Eiffel Tower. Certain that Hawk would jump him as soon as he jumped on board one of the riverboats, he resigned himself to the imbroglio at hand. "If your hapless victim leapt off the tower, how did his Montmartre beret manage to stay on his head during the ill-fated plunge?"

Hawk ran his pen back and forth across his teeth like a stick across the slats of a picket fence. "Place the beret, the Tour de France shades, the champagne bottle, and the rest of his bits and bobs on those steps beneath the left leg of the tower. That will show premeditated murder. Self-murder, that is. Leave the *boules* ball in the sand to your right. Make sure you roll the bottle across his fingers to plant some prints."

"But we drank from that champagne bottle, he didn't."

"Trust me, the cops won't even notice."

"Trusting you was my first mistake. You are evil personified."

Hawk bowed at the waist while swinging his pocket watch like a hypnotist's tool. "Roll the bottle across his palm a few times. We haven't much time."

"Was he right-handed or left-handed?"

"Didn't you notice?" he laughed as if murder were mere dinner theater to him. "I handed him drink after drink with my right hand, but he took them with his left."

"Now what?" bleated the accidental accomplice, his hands shaking.

"Now we plant this pen and paper which I got from that girl in the crimson cloak and clogs. Little Red Riding Hood was only too happy to help the Big, Bad Wolf." He enjoyed the ease with which he intimidated his comrade into compliance. "I'll make the suicide note short and sweet, so my handwriting doesn't come back to haunt me."

"If this murder doesn't come back to haunt you, your handwriting won't." James scoured his eyes with his fists, trying to erase the indelible image of death at his feet. "I'm not touching anything else. You can waltz his beret over to that bench all by your sweet self."

"I didn't realize you wanted to be alone with the *corpus delicti* when the cops arrive."

James slipped the beret off the corpse but refused to plant any prints. Hawk scribbled "Goodbye cruel world!" on the stationery along with a French phrase he created just for the occasion: *"Joie de mort!"* Using his gloved hand, he rolled the dead man's fingerprints on to the bottle, taking care not to get any champagne on his dapper coat. The name on the pen suddenly caught the killer's eye. "Civitas Dei? This must be the name of Little Red Riding Hood's hotel."

James' blood ran cold. He knew Civitas Dei was no hotel. Civitas Dei was the college he and his sister Danielle had attended. He wondered if there was any chance Hawk hadn't noticed that name was written on the back of his jacket. He decided to play along. "Civitas Dei is Latin, not French, so Little Red is probably staying at one of those student dives in the Latin Quarter."

"The authorities will assume this was also a student dive," Hawk snorted.

James scanned the tower for his sister. "Where is Little Red Riding Hood now?"

"Stealing her way up a down staircase, or stealing something else, no doubt."

Unable to spot his sister on the superstructure, James asked Hawk to let him see the pen.

Hawk thrust it into the corpse instead. "They'll think the pen pierced his leg during the fatal plunge. You must admit, this isn't something you'd do to yourself."

James bent over to keep from retching. "I get the sick feeling you're enjoying this."

"Your feelings are your problem." Hawk tucked the suicide note inside the bottle.

James glared at the *boules* ball. The fact that it resembled a shot-put also made him sick to his stomach since shot-putting was his speciality. "Tell me you haven't done this before."

"*Au contraire.* I've never pierced a man's thigh with a Civitas Dei pen at sunset on the twentieth of February under the Eiffel Tower with two point seven liters of Billecart-Salmon in my system."

Having succumbed to the habit of letting others run his life, James couldn't think for himself in the face of death. He carried the bottle, the beret, and the sunglasses across the sand like a lily-livered errand boy, not realizing the suicide note would also implicate him since Hawk penned it on Civitas Dei stationery. Sitting down on the cold stone landing, James tried to wipe his fingerprints off each item. His head swirling and his heart hammering, he knew Hawk's eyes were fixed on him like lasers. *Why should I be afraid? I didn't do it. But the cops won't believe I didn't do it since Hawk took the trouble to frame me. I can't believe he got a Civitas Dei pen from my sister! If I go to the cops, they might accidentally arrest her!*

The befuddled jock rose to his toes calmly and quietly, but his eyes tripped on a blue sign attached to a pole. Sweat broke across his upper lip as he realized the letters formed a word he didn't want to read: POLICE. Shaking like a bed with a dollar in it, he discovered the Parisians had built a cop shop under the Eiffel Tower and were no doubt misunderstanding his every move.

James pivoted sharply, only to find Hawk laughing with unabashed amusement. Realizing the degree to which he had been set up, he ran for his life.

✠

Having thoroughly enjoyed her visit to the first level of the Eiffel Tower, Danielle Seabright tiptoed up the latticed iron steps to the second level of the Parisian candelabra, despite the fact the staircase had been closed earlier. Pleased that she was getting something for nothing again, she found her luck changing when the "borrowed" *boules* ball tumbled out of her red cape and bounced its way down the metal steps beneath her. Knowing the noise would arouse suspicion, she shrugged off the toy as if it were mere jetsam and dashed up the iron incline like a cat on coffee. Her clogs spun her around nervously, however, when she heard voices trailing behind her. The bouncing ball had obviously told an employee what she didn't want him to hear.

The guard gave chase, shouting in tones not suitable for the funeral of a truly dead person, while his whistle added an international interpretation. Little Red Riding Hood soon arrived on the second level, leaving it to the French officials to update the land speed record.

Fireworks sprayed the top of the Eiffel Tower while huge spotlights swept across its great iron legs. Too panicked to enjoy the dramatic display, the caped adventurer tried to fly south for the winter as soon as an elevator would accommodate her. The line for the ride down was longer than the line for wine, however, so she hid inside a souvenir photo booth. Poking her head through the wooden cut-out of the tourist trap at no great distance from her, she was more than a little surprised to see the camera flash at her. Apparently someone had overfed the machine on a prior visit. Two souvenir photos spat out at her. Not liking that she was alone in the pictures, she stuffed them in her pocket along with her ticket stub.

Her butt then nudged against something on the corner of the seat. *Someone left a wallet in here? Thank You, God! I'll only take what I need...on second thought, what I need is a drink, so I'll take a little extra.* She pocketed enough euros to soar to the top of the tower after a suds.

Her heart racing like a metronome at a ska concert, she peeked outside the photo booth curtain. Directly across from her makeshift hideaway stood a fast food boutique whose patrons were preoccupied with the ordering of overpriced entrees. Apparently no one considered it a vital career move to nab her, so she reversed sides on her cape, knowing the red side was too garish for an uneventful getaway. *Only the fashion police will arrest me now,* she laughed. When the libations line was down to one un-uniformed customer, she snagged a glass of grog and returned to her hidey hole to savor it in peace until she was sure the coast was clear.

Ten minutes later she purchased a ticket for a trip to the top of the tower, culpable but quite pleased with herself just the same. When the elevator door swept open, the stunning view of Paris captivated her in a way that nothing ever had. Twirling like an off-Broadway actress in a garage rendition of the *Sound of Music*, she spun around the iron pinnacle until her eyes had taken in all the sights they could stand: the golden Gothic towers of Notre Dame, the luminous glass pyramid of the Louvre, the colorful whirl of the Arc de Triomphe, and the ice cream domes of Sacre Coeur on the hilltop horizon. *No wonder they say good Americans, when they die, go to Paris! But oh, how I hate seeing special things without someone special at my side! I have to meet someone soon for a foreign fling* sans *a ring.*

Seabright lounged against the railing to fantasize about the future, knowing the anticipation could be an adventure in itself. Not wanting to lose her quixotic vision, she closed her eyes to preserve her rhapsodic images, when suddenly a siren pierced the air below her, a siren which grew louder and louder with every beat of her heart. Her gaze followed the floodlit Seine until she realized the flashing lights were heading straight for the great iron candlestick itself.

Having stolen the *boules* ball, not to mention her access to the second level, she shifted her bookbag underneath her cape to make herself look pregnant, then she pushed and shoved her way on to the elevator as was the local custom. *The French wouldn't call the cops just because I borrowed a few bucks from a guy's wallet, would they?*

One of the self-portraits from the photo booth tumbled out of her cape, but her impromptu pregnancy prevented her from reaching the floor to retrieve it as the crowded elevator lunged toward ground level.

Seabright scanned the Parisian premises to the extent possible while descending the metal menagerie in a cage. Her eyes were drawn to a macabre tourist attraction around which people were gathering like flies. A body was lying in the sand at the bottom of the tower with a ball next to it, quite possibly a *boules* ball. Her legs suddenly felt as wobbly as a clown on a unicycle.

Meanwhile, three box-capped *gendarmes* attempted to dispel the parasitic passers-by who were taking pictures of the corpse as if it were the latest addition to a wax museum. A militaristic nun enjoyed greater success in crowd control by clambering on to a park bench to preside over the emergency like a Napolean with a bun. In order to facilitate a hasty retreat, Little Red Riding Hood gave birth to her bookbag without the help of a meddling midwife. Then she blended into the bustling crowd on Quai Branly as the candlestick loomed over her like a dark cloud that threatened to ruin her European vacation.

CHAPTER TWO

Café Athens, Latin Quarter
Noon 21 February

Passionate yet playful, Parker created a parking space when he spotted his niece at a Left Bank café. It wasn't the warmest day for a ride, but his Harley had become year-round transportation when he decided to call Paris home. "Little Red Riding Hood!"

The cocky collegian didn't want to be seen with her uncle, but Seabright acquiesced to a half hug while checking out his motorcycle. After all, he was letting her stay at his Montmartre apartment, so she figured she owed him something, but it overlooked a cemetery, so she discounted her gratitude accordingly. "My outfit isn't as silly as yours," she said as he doffed an Alpine hat, complete with feather. "Is this why you're known as the German American in Paris?"

"*Ja oui!*" Parker laughed. "I guess I'm garish to a fault, more nutty than natty."

"Vogue-vague and *tres* trendless, I'd say," she sneered.

"Alas, each of us exhibits an affinity for alliteration!" Born with a rack of teeth too stiff for his gentle smile, Parker exuded warmth and understanding, but he didn't seem to understand the French dress code. Adorned in a Harley jacket and Bavarian chaps–*lederhosen* with the crotch cut out–he fit into the chic Paris environs like a grizzly on a fashion runway. "I thought I'd died and gone to heaven when I first came to Paris because Notre Dame was right in front of me when I came up out of the subway. What does Danielle think of the City of Light?"

"I like it better when the lights go out." She threw her billowing black locks over her shoulder to demonstrate how grown up she was.

"I'd rather you didn't call me Danielle while I'm in Paris. I transposed my first and last names to enjoy a change of identity overseas. If the authorities ever question me, I figure it will look like an honest mistake," she tee-heed.

Parker's teddy bear face tried to tee-hee. "Did people mistake Danielle for Daniel?"

"Do I look like a Daniel?" She struck a seductive pose capable of tempting fate, among other bandits. "At least I'm not pretending I have an Ivy League name like my boring brother James. He's using his middle name as his last name while in Europe, so he's calling himself James Woodlawn. I guess Seabright is too sissy of a last name for a big time jock."

"The sap in our family tree doesn't seem to flow with any nomenclatural purity." He sat down at her tiny table under a fluttering green awning. "Some of the pavement cafes up on Rue Saint Jacques are enclosed in glass, so we wouldn't have to freeze our buns off," he hinted.

"I don't want to dine in a glorified greenhouse that has one of those stupid blackboard menus on the sidewalk. Those outdoor cafes look like indoor aquariums." Her words dripped with sarcasm, thinking it sounded sophisticated.

It was too cold to eat outside, but Parker knew that if eating at a sidewalk cafe was what made her feel as if she were in Paris, he wanted her to enjoy all she could of it while she was young, so the memories would keep her warm as she grew old. Memories of Europe were keeping him plenty warm on many a cold night with many a cold soul.

Seabright fidgeted with the menu, hoping her uncle would order first, so he wouldn't realize what a Philistine she was, despite her advertisements to the contrary. Sensing she was about to order a helping of humble pie, Parker suggested, "Why not start with a *horse divorce*?"

She couldn't help but smile, but then she rescinded her facial friendliness, knowing any show of emotion would give him an unpredictable power over her. "All I know is that pain is not on my menu." She rattled the ice in her glass, telling him she had already killed some pain.

"*Pain* is on my menu," Parker quipped, his whiskers wiggling. "*Pain* is French for bread. This is the rambunctious Latin Quarter. *Epater les bourgeois* are the watchwords over here, which guarantees there will be plenty to watch. That means 'deliberately disturb the middle class.' They may not even serve us since we aren't appropriately inappropriately attired."

"You are plenty inappropriately, believe me. You are more chichi than chic, Parker."

"Does this hat not say I habituate the haberdasheries of *haute couture*?"

She looked down her nose at him to consummate her snottiness. "You're not serious."

"Not often. Taking yourself seriously is a serious burden. As for which entrees are edible at this eatery, I wouldn't sink my molars into any dead cows. A gal pal sent her side of beef back three times. Apparently, she was under the impression they would cook it for her. Each time the waiter just fluttered his hand, pirouetted, then sashayed off looking very offended."

She reminded him of his sins to better excuse her own. "Was this gal pal your ex?"

"No, an acquaintance who threw her own get-acquainted party at my expense. She's one of those me-first flakes who claims she ruled Egypt in a past life, no doubt as Cleopatra. She's taking a correspondence course to become a cat psychic, if her demons don't eat her alive first."

Seabright snickered after trying not to. "I didn't expect you to be so honest."

"I can be honest to a fault, but I'll not bore you further with my fabled foibles. I hear you had your heart set on the Portuguese coast? Something about an art study in the Algarve?"

"*Tres* true, but Jezebel grabbed the grant for that foreign classroom while pursuing a pulpit to promote perversion. That disingenuous woman is genuinely deceiving people."

"Some people want to be deceived. The serpent has his servants, some of whom hide the blackness of their rebellion behind white robes. But don't blame God for what she did. That's a snakebite in itself." He adjusted the strap on his Bavarian suspenders. "The Bible encourages us to expose false teachers, so why don't you channel your energy in that direction?"

Seabright wrenched her face like a constipated gargoyle. "Why? Users are just losers."

"The devil is trying to take advantage of your injury. Satan was the original ambulance chaser. He dispatches a dump truck full of resentment and revenge to every accident site; unwary victims choose to nosh on his poisonous provisions. However, virtue *is* the best revenge."

"Virtue is boring." She snuck a Café Athens coaster into her backpack as he said grace.

"She'll get what's coming to her. Nobody gets away with anything. The fires of hell are going to burn hot for heretics. Have you heard of that temple tune *Boomerang?*"

"I don't like Christian music. Neither does Robespierre."

"Robespierre?"

"A priest I met for drinks last night."

"He's a minister, and he doesn't like Christian music? Doesn't he realize there's going to be a lot of Christian music in heaven?" Parker raised his eyebrows twice to tweak the irony.

"He doesn't concern himself much with heaven or hell. The Chateau Bleu we shared was heavenly, however. The French name their wine after their favorite *chateau.* I like a man who likes a cork in his lunch." She chuckled at the picture of the chef on the napkin ring who looked as if he had eaten his way to the top of the food chain. "A glass of wine takes the edge off."

"Two glasses makes the edge more appealing. Speaking of edges, someone went over the edge of the Eiffel Tower last night." He plastered his *pain* with cheese butter as she crossed her eyes until they hurt. "*Le Bon Dieu vous le rendra.* The Good Lord will repay you."

She jerked backwards as if hit by a bat. "Repay me for what, pray tell?"

"God will repay you for being bumped out of your position in Portugal. As for shuffling off this mortal coil, do you know anything about that death at the Iron Lady last night?"

"Why would I know anything about it?" Seabright sizzled.

Parker studied her trembling hands. "You were in town. I was in transit."

"James was in town, too. Why don't you ask him? Are we nosy to a fault, too?" She sat on her hands to keep them from shaking. "Since when does James stay out *tres* late?"

"He's a big boy. He does what he wants to."

"So do I." She snatched the drink menu. "My bland brother stumbled in as the cock crowed, as shaken as a suds on a Harley. That's not like him. James lets life happen to him. He could only be spontaneous if he knew ahead of time what to be spontaneous about. Why live a life that so closely resembles death? Robespierre says we must live all of our lives in this time."

"He must have forgot about eternity." Parker tied his orange Harley bandanna around his neck like a bank robber's bib. "Funny how your Robespierre thinks just like Goethe."

Her mouth twitched with equal amounts of embarrassment and agitation, not willing to let a relative challenge her intentions when said relative was still a relative stranger. "I find love where love finds me. Priests have always fascinated me."

"Help me understand this fascination."

She looked away from his honest eyes. "Perhaps it's the illicit that solicits me."

"You and everyone else." He closed his mouth to facilitate the biting of his tongue.

"Just imagine what a rhapsodic interlude would mean to a man deprived of passion."

"You're tempting fate and a father?"

"I thought I was supposed to put my fate in the Father's hands."

"That logic is so tortured I should call Amnesty International." A waiter tended to the needs of the French poodle seated nearest them.

"How do you know this guy is a priest?"

"I asked him if he was one. He doesn't exactly act like one, but why should he have to?"

"Was he wearing a cross, a collar, or a papal tiara, perhaps?"

"No. He's not into the trappings of traditional churchianity. Neither am I. He looks like a Bohemian Bolshevik, not some pompous pulpiteer with an ego the size of Siberia."

"He doesn't sound like any priest I know. He could have tossed that body from the Eiffel Tower before it *was* a body. I would wake up and smell the *café au lait*. Better safe than sorry."

"Safety is for cowards. I've been playing it safe my whole life."

"But you know he's a priest, and forbidden fruit will make you sick."

"I'd rather be sick for a season than dead my whole life."

"That's the fallacy of false dilemma. Your choice isn't limited to being sick from forbidden fruit or dead from the lack of it. Speaking of the dead, did you see the *corpus delicti*?"

"You lawyers are such Latin lovers. My guess is the *corpus* in question was a jumper."

"You couldn't jump off the Eiffel Tower if you tried. The netting is wrapped tighter than the wire on a teenager's teeth. It's hard to throw a ball off there, let alone a body."

"Why did you mention a ball? Did someone find a ball?"

His green velveteen suspenders shrugged. "The paper said something about a champagne bottle, a suicide note—oh, and a pen that was lodged in the guy's leg."

She swallowed a fur ball of fear. "But a ball wouldn't fit through the webbing, right?"

"A jock like James could probably launch one through the lattice. Why do you ask?"

"Is it illegal to ask questions in France?" She cracked her knuckles, all ten at once.

Parker stroked his salt-and-pepper beard, evaluating her evasiveness. "I smell a rat, or at least rat droppings. If you're in some kind of trouble, I'd like to help you."

Craving a drink to drown her fears and fuel her fantasies, she flagged down the *garcon.*

Parker winced. "Have you tried a mint-kissed mineral water or *chocolat pain*?"

"Where's the buzz in that?" She opened her map of Montmartre to avoid his kind eyes.

"I like to remember the good times I'm having, like climbing the Eiffel for the first time."

She fondled the libations list. "Why are you trying to place me at the scene of the crime?"

"Crime?" He looked around for a newspaper. "It wasn't a suicide?"

"Who knows? I can't read French." A yellow Lab dressed up in a Monet scarf ordered a stack of ham pancakes, promising not to leave a tip on the sidewalk this time.

"Did you know I studied French, then the missions board mailed my butt to Bernkastel?"

"I heard you were shipped there because 'the other woman' was here."

"She was here a little there a little, but the board didn't know. God knew, however. God always knows. Now I'm a modern missionary. I pay my own way and pick up the tab for a thousand other missionaries—paper missionaries, that is. Did you know the Sorbonne was the first university in Europe, and it not only devoted itself to theology but printed Gospel leaflets on its first press? I don't leave home without them."

"I tucked Civitas Dei Scripture cards into newspapers at the airport, but then I figured I owed myself a real vacation, so I left the entire stack of them in a duty free shop next to boxes of chocolates that had cute little pictures of Paris printed on each candy."

"I always carry a Bible since you never know when the man you meet on the Metro is about to meet his Maker. More than once, a person has died soon after I gave him the Gospel."

"You're also morose to a fault. Who else likes an apartment that overlooks a cemetery?"

"It keeps me focused on Forever like Capuchin cemeteries that display corpses like canvases. Paris is known as the City of Life, but there's a good helping of death here, too. You just have to know where to look for it. Rome isn't the only city with catacombs. Paris also has a nice spread. My view of Montmartre's mortuary has served as a poignant *memento mori* for a motorcycle missionary like me. It's also a visual reminder to my guests that they, too, will die."

"I bet it's a real conversation piece, just like your clothes," she razzed him.

Incorrigibly playful, he curtsied to show off his Bavarian bikerwear.

Not wanting to admit she started tying her black velvet vest like a corset when she arrived in Paris so she wouldn't look so much like an Israeli folk dancer, she changed the subject before her clothes were called into question. "Robespierre is going to take me to see miles of underground wine cellars on a castles 'n' casks tour. Just because you quit drinking doesn't mean the whole world has to quit." She chewed her lip like a wad of gum. "Why did you quit?"

"I couldn't do the math. One plus one more equaled one too many. Augustine said total abstinence is easier than perfect moderation. A pastor is supposed to be man of substance, but I became a man of substance abuse. I rationalized my way right out of the pulpit. Bunyan warned that said sins don't travel alone, and I found alcohol to be an *agent provocateur.*"

"Maybe I like being a little provocative." She twirled her foot coquettishly, but only the dog noticed. "Robespierre taught me a French phrase: *In vino veritas,* in wine there is truth."

"It's Latin, but there's some truth to it. There is more half-truth, however. Write down what you're thinkin' next time you're drinkin'. I think you'll be unpleasantly surprised."

She stared into his attentive green eyes, unaccustomed to such generosity of spirit. "I thought you'd lecture me with abandon about absinthe and all alcohol less colorful."

"Your own life will lecture you if I don't." He gave her a Metro map and phrase book.

"Dostoyevsky said, 'Don't be too frightened even at your evil actions.'"

"What evil have you committed that is now frightening you?" Parker investigated.

"Nothing...yet." The *garcon* dumped off their drinks, preferring the pets to the people.

The German American in Paris offered her a *petit pain*, but she wasn't interested in his buns. He went fishing to find out what was so fishy about her attitude. "I don't know about you, but I find it harder to repent of the sins I plan to commit than the ones I already quit committing."

"That's your problem." She hated that Paris' classy café awnings also fit pop-up campers.

The motorcycle missionary dug out a biker Bible for a waiter who liked to make people wait. "Are you a Christian?"

"I was. I think I still am," she guffawed behind the menu. "Okay, I admit I've been doing some things I shouldn't, but I want to see the far country for myself, at least from the suburbs."

"The suburbs and the far country share the same zip code." He offered her his biker gloves as he blew on his hands. "Tell me more about this priest. Is Robespierre his real name?"

"Of course. Why would a stranger lie to me?"

"Telling people what they want to hear has its advantages."

"You're forgetting, he's a man of God. He also happens to be an artist, not to mention a professor at the Sorbonne."

"Be careful. Those pick-up lines have won more women than Napolean won wars."

"Don't tell me to be careful while I'm in Paris. For once in my life I want to live my life with reckless abandon *a corps perdu,* as Robespierre would say, to the very loss of my body."

"And to the loss of your soul? Emerson said life is a festival only to the wise, but festivals don't have to be sinfests. I 'festival' on my bike." He rotated his wrists as if revving his Harley.

"Robespierre is a festival of fashions in his leggings and knickers, but he has some pirate in him too. He has thick Lenin eyebrows with a ring in one brow, whiskers like a broom, and womanly eyes. He's very charming, at least in his own mind." A snicker escaped unfettered as she pocketed the souvenir matches, not afraid of any fire she herself would start.

"Where did you meet a guy wearing Parisian pantyhose? The Marais?"

"No, Rue Valentin. 'Valentin' is probably French for 'valentine,' so I took that as an immortal wink of Providence that I was meant to be with an artist for a season."

"Painting the bathroom doesn't make you an artist."

A crocodile smirk disfigured her childlike face. "You can't tell a Monet from a bidet."

"I can since I moved to Paris. Art is the blood of the French people. I'm just trying to spare you the pain. They're all artists when the bars close. He's celibate, so that's a problem."

"It's not a problem for me. I don't think priests should have to be celibate."

"It might be a problem for God." Parker saw his own life flash before his eyes. "'What a man likes to do, that he thinks right to do.' Goethe was right about that."

"Goethe also said, 'Live dangerously and you live right.' *Touche!*"

The German American in Paris watched the bubbles pop in his *l'eau gazeuse*, glad it would not serve as a segue to sin. "I love a tall glass of *l'eau gazeuse* after a long ride."

"What is *l'eau gazeuse*?"

"Water. Bubbling mineral water, to be exact."

Seabright burst out laughing, but the anger coursing through her veins soon turned her face into a cold visage that would have made a lovely addition to Mount Rushmore. "When Robespierre is through with the Church, some things won't be sins any more."

Parker's eyes popped with incredulity. "Is he penning his own Parchments?"

"Men wrote the Bible, so men can rewrite it. He's just updating our definition of sin."

Personable Parker gave her a list of France's Top 25 Attractions, twelve of which were cheeses and thirteen of which were breads, but she refused to eat. "Revisionism is just rebellion on paper, and rebellion is as the sin of witchcraft. Heretics mistake apostasy for higher education."

"I'm looking for love, not education. I already got me an education," she laughed. "My priest got jealous when he thought James was my boyfriend."

Parker twirled his goblet. "Did James go out with you two last night?"

"No, but my best picture of me has James in it. Robespierre wanted to see all of my pictures, even my passport. I was pleasantly surprised, because my last pastor was hellbent on lecturing everybody while listening to nobody. Then again, it was the devil who ordained her."

"Did Robespierre show you his passport and pictures?"

"Why should he?"

"Why shouldn't he? If he wants to know your business, you ought to know his."

"Contrary to popular belief, priests are people too." She tried to corner him with the café table since she felt rather cornered herself, but a round table rendered cornering impossible.

"Don't accept double standards. Disease develops in the shade—and shady characters."

"There's nothing shady about him; he's turned the light on for me. He's *tres* original. He told me to question everything and watch for error, even in Holy Scripture. Isn't that profound?"

"Profoundly cynical. If he's so original, why does he parrot Peter Abelard?"

"Great minds think alike; great minds think alot," she replied with an economy of effort.

"I wouldn't be surprised to find out your priest is a plagiarist, plumber, and expatriate."

Her porcelain smile shattered at the impact of his accusations. "What's an expatriate?"

"Someone who lives in a foreign country, often for suspicious reasons. That's a red flag."

"You assume he has something to hide, and you haven't even met him."

"Can I meet him? If he has nothing to hide, let him prove it by hiding nothing."

Seabright crossed her arms like swords. "You wouldn't understand his theology."

"Why? Is his theology ornithology—for the birds? Or seismology—cracked?" He waved the Café Athens cocktail napkin. "I see another red flag, Little Red Riding Hood."

"Don't judge. There are many theologies in the Bible."

"People who say 'don't judge' don't know the Bible. Neither are there many theologies in the Bible. That's a red flag, too. One more flag and we'll have ourselves a parade."

"Not everything is in the Bible."

"Not everything isn't. Soren Kierkegaard wrote: 'It is not the obscure passages in Scripture that bind you but the ones you understand. With these you are to comply at once.'"

Her half moon smile vanished like a lunar eclipse. Parker reached across the table to squeeze her hand. "This priest is probably no axe murderer, but if he sinks the boat of your faith, you'll be easy prey for any one of Satan's sharks. I don't want that to happen. The Eiffel Tower killer wouldn't even have to cross your path...you'd find yourself on his."

CHAPTER THREE

Poste de Police, Tour Eiffel
1:20 p.m. 21 February

"Who is she, and why was her picture found in the wallet of the Eiffel Tower victim?" asked the crotchety Parisian police officer with the pencil mustache whose eraser smile delighted in erasing the smiles of others. "While we are reviewing the facts of this case that was dropped at our doorstep, pardon the pun, tell me the name of these silly shoes the suspect is wearing."

"Clogs. The Dutch wear them, but she is friendly like an American. I remind you that hers isn't the only face in that Christmas-at-the-beach photograph that we found in the dead man's wallet," countered the younger, less cantankerous cop whose pleasure did not consist in depriving others of their pleasure. "The young man standing next to Little Red Riding Hood is wearing a Civitas Dei College jacket, the same kind of jacket a suspect was wearing under the Eiffel the night of the murder. The American male wearing the Civitas Dei jacket is the same suspect who placed the beret, the bottle and the glasses on the park bench along with that bogus suicide note."

"Where do you get that he is American? The name on his jacket is not written in English."

"'College' is written in English. I bet Little Red and the college boy are both Americans."

"Then they are probably in on this together."

"But they are not traveling together. They remain separated all evening."

The semi-senile but completely cranky cop jammed some brown flakes into his pipe. "She was on the tower at the same time he was underneath the tower, so I suspect they are working as a team. Why else would they split up when visiting such a popular sight?"

The young cop glanced at his new arm patch which told tourists he spoke English, or something close to it. "She looks harmless enough to me, probably a student lacking in money more than morals. Maybe this man in the photo is a classmate. Obviously, she does not prefer his company, or she would not have ascended the pinnacle of romance without him."

"The security camera shows she changed clothes on level two," snarled the grumpy *gendarme,* "and she suddenly became pregnant on level three. These are suspicious acts."

The kinder, gentler cop loosened his tie as if not entirely comfortable with suspecting everyone of everything all the time. "What evidence leads you to suspect her?"

"If it is not obvious to you, perhaps I should arrest you for impersonating an officer." He sparked his lighter then drew the flame into the bowl of the pipe. "She is pretending to be pregnant. Why? Also, she does not stroll like a tourist but lurches from niche to niche like a naughty cat. Did you notice what she does when the guard sees her? She draws her red hood over her head and presses her face to a viewing scope."

"It is cold atop the Eiffel, so a hood is good. That she pays for a panoramic view is not suspicious in and of itself. It would be suspicious had she not. I still enjoy the scopes."

The crank blew smoke into the junior officer's face to see if he would do anything about it. "If she is innocent, why has she not come forward? She probably ran off to the Riviera."

His shoulders froze mid-shrug in the up position. "This murder just happened yesterday. Perhaps the girl does not read the papers, or perhaps she cannot even read French." He twisted his can-like *kepi* hat back and forth against his skull to help him concentrate. "Perhaps she spilled a *citron presse* on her cape and turned it inside out so no one would see the stain."

"But she exited the Eiffel elevator not only having reversed her cloak but pretending to be pregnant, as well. Is the 'baby' something she stole from one of the Eiffel's gift shops?"

Half the age of his prickly elder yet twice the man, the rookie cop examined the footage from a ground camera. "Look at this camera angle. The girl gave birth to a book bag."

"But why did she do these strange things? People do things for a reason, unless they are insane, and they are often insane for a reason." He chewed on his pipe as smoke swirled up his nose like a chimney. "A news photo shows this woman leaning over the victim's body. She may have been stealing the contents of his wallet since the contents are missing. She is also a thief."

"I would not jump to such conclusions without a safety net, sir. A telephoto lens makes objects look closer than they really are, so this dark-haired beauty might not really have been leaning over anyone. I can make the Place de la Concorde obelisk look as if it's inside the Arch de Triumphe even though we both know the Champs Elysees separates the two monuments."

"But we also have a written complaint from a *fromagerie.* This caped crusader stole a Camembert cheese from his shop on her second day in our country. When confronted, she said she was just borrowing it. Who borrows cheese? It is as likely that she will return the cheese as a babysitter is likely to return to a crowded theater to retrieve a dirty diaper."

"How do we know this lonely girl is that cheesy woman?"

"Cape, clogs and the cannibalizing of our language." He smiled with malicious delight as if auditioning for the Riddler in a *Batman* movie.

"She may have been confused. In America they do not purchase a ticket before they take a product off the shelf. They pick first, pay second."

The crusty curmudgeon rifled through the photos on his desk as if he had a losing hand in poker. "These other images from a security camera show her coming up a roped off staircase, so she is obviously entering level two without paying. I now have two proofs that she is a thief."

The more merciful man cross-questioned the surly cross examiner: "Were you never young and poor? I climbed up the down staircase many times when I was broke. It is considered a rite of passage in the Chaillot Quarter. If this girl murdered this guy, why did she not remove her picture from his wallet? She must have known it would implicate her."

"Maybe she didn't know it was in there. What excuse do you make for the *boules* ball?"

"I am not familiar with that aspect of the case."

"Then it is time you two were introduced." The gruff old sod poked the end of his pipe into his nose as if certifiably bored. "A gypsy sashayed into our cop shop to inform us that the woman in question showed off her stolen *boules* ball when they were in line for the elevator."

"How does he know she stole it?"

"He saw her steal it."

"Why would anyone bother reporting something like that? Would you take time to tattle on a tourist? Maybe this petty rat is throwing the scent off his own pelt."

"He suspects she is more than a thief. Perhaps this gypsy has a crystal ball. In this photo, you see the *boules* ball in her hands. In the next photo, she sticks it in her cape. When she sneaks to level two, there is no ball in her hand. We found a *boules* ball like hers by the corpse."

"So, you think this girl carried a concealed weapon up the tower, and that concealed weapon was a lawn bowling ball? I would like to see the ballistics report on a theory like that."

He wriggled his mustache as if determined to sneeze on his handsome subordinate. "We have attempted to preserve the evidence, but the toxicology report is not yet available."

"Has the coroner determined the time of death and whether or not the man actually died at the Eiffel? He could have been dropped off here after expiring elsewhere."

"The victim was alive at the tower. Dead men do not carry on conversations."

The novice officer resolved that his uniform would never look as spent as a tourist's wallet. "Why do you suspect the girl and not her college companion? They were photographed together so they obviously know each other. Just because she is a thief does not mean she is a murderer. As for the *boules* ball, I doubt anyone would drop it like a marble from such heights."

"They were traveling on a wagon of wine, so anything is possible."

"I checked, and the girl with the cape and clogs was not on the chateau and champagne tour. There is therefore a hole in your theory. You may exit through it now if you wish."

The grouch with the grub-like line over his lip did not appreciate having his authority challenged by a junior officer, a senior officer, or anyone not an officer. He rapped his pipe against the table like a gavel. "My cousin was playing *boules* at Dog Park yesterday, and a ball disappeared from their court. I have good reason to believe she stole it. The gypsy tattler saw her steal it, then our victim was bashed over the head with it. Her motive was probably money."

"Good reasons go bad if you stick to the facts. What do you plan to say to her when you interrogate her? Young lady, a process of elimination tells us that 2 + 2 = U?"

"There is more. The fake suicide note, written in English, has a botched French phrase in it that is typical of a pretentious American student. It reads '*joie de mort*' instead of '*joie de vivre.*' The English are not so eager to imitate us as the Americans."

The youngster hated the way the police profession deified cynicism. "How can we be sure the victim did not commit suicide? There have been 27 suicides from the top of the tower."

"Not lately. The body could not have fallen through the iron webbing and land where it did. Draw a line straight up from the corpse and you hit the dinner show on the second level."

"Maybe the victim was thrown from the tower."

The duffer howled with laughter, trying to accomplish with condescension what he could easily have accomplished with courtesy. "If he was thrown, why did his jacket not burst open after the 900 foot plunge, and why did his glasses not break upon impact? There are other questions. Why did the autopsy detect poison in the victim's blood? You don't bother poisoning someone if you plan on throwing him off a tower. And why did the bottle found next to the fake suicide note have champagne in it if the victim had been drinking wine?"

"The fingerprints on the bottle were upside down, and few people I know are able to drink from a bottle pointing toward the ground, so the victim's prints may have been planted." He flashed his unnaturally even teeth. "I think our murderer has mistaken volatility for virility."

"Who cares what you think? Find this clogged girl and ask her where she was between the hours of four and seven, what business she has in Paris, who she knows in Paris, and when she plans to leave Paris, but do not let her leave Paris, of course. Post the necessary bulletins."

A curl of smoke surrounded the junior officer's nose. He whisked it away but not in an obvious way such as would have invited more smoke. "What if this girl is not the killer?"

"In my expert opinion, the killer is either a tourist, a drunk, a student unfamiliar with the Eiffel, or all of the above, as is most likely the case. I do not doubt we are hunting for a killer who is playing dumb because she is smart." The argumentative, abdominous cop resented having his routine altered, preferring to remain as unproductive as a stump.

"Young females are rarely serial killers, neither do they play games with foreign police when traveling alone," countered the unfat uniformed officer. "Pilfering like hers often begins at an early age as a reaction to a mother who uses the men in her life to punish her. Kleptos quickly discard what they steal, reinforcing the cycle of guilt, envy and unlovedness that precipitated the self-defeating behavior, not unlike the gorging and disgorging cycles of a bulimic."

The smoker studied him with a jaundiced eye. "This is not a serial killer."

"Why not? All the fingers point to a predator. Predators are narcissistic, and the killer chose a high visibility location, symptomatic of a narcissist. This breed chooses its victim from those who volunteer to help him, then he positions himself to earn her trust. Such monsters are so overconfident they do not even entertain the notion of negative consequences."

The crab picked at his pipe, too preoccupied with his toy to validate junior's insights.

"Psychopaths are easily bored and have a deep pathological attachment to their victims, unless they thrill kill, then any stranger will do. Killing is a cannibalistic catharsis for them."

His face groaned with grumpiness. "Is this what they teach at police school nowadays?"

"Among other things," the rookie replied calmly, gaining his own confidence. "Revenge is the killer's reason for living and others' dying. He punishes people for not loving him."

"What evidence suggests any of this fascinating hogwash?"

"Historical evidence, for starters. If this is a professional trying to look like an amateur, the murder is probably personal since he killed at close range. I'd like to review the frames that show the man in the wool coat. His business-as-usual demeanor is disturbing and could prove to be damning. Serial killers are comfortable with killing and do not overkill, so a cavalier attitude is often his calling card. The crime scene will tell us whether or not this was an overkill. He may also have taken a trophy from the victim, as serials often do."

He chewed his pipe stem like a beaver, hoping to annoy his more competent young coworker. While contemplating the ways in which he could play with his pipe, his tobacco, and the resulting smoke for the duration of his shift, the unkempt codger added, "The letterhead on the fake suicide note is imprinted with the Civitas Dei logo, as is the pen that was found in the victim's thigh. Coincidentally, the name printed on this other suspect's jacket also reads Civitas Dei College, so begin your search by finding out which Civitas Dei students recently purchased passports to Paris, along with airline tickets, both used and yet-to-be used."

CHAPTER FOUR

The Left Bank, Paris
1:20 p.m. 21 February

Parker dangled his keys in front of Seabright. "How about a two-wheeled tour of Paris?"

"I'm game. Maybe we'll run into Robespierre while we're zooming and vrroommming."

"Literally, I hope." Not appreciating her attachment to the religious rebel, Parker paid the café tab then escorted his niece to his Harley, helmet in hand. "Doing Paris on a bike is different than doing Paris in a car. You'll understand why we call cars 'cages' when you feel the breeze caress your face as you cross the Seine, and you'll notice every contour of cobblestone in the old quarter. Neither will you miss the aromas that you do in a car–*bifteck* sizzling on outdoor grills, bread baking in *boulangeries*, and chestnuts roasting on carnival carts. Sounds are clearer when you're not enclosed in glass, too, like all those sexy saxophones in the Latin Quarter and the sentimental accordions of Montmartre. On a motorcycle, you will experience Paris in ways the guidebook never dreamed of."

With a twist of the throttle, their transportation was ready to roll. Parker revved his engine more than was necessary, knowing the roar of the pipes would add to her fun. He then whisked her up and down one bank of the Seine and then the other, crossing the bridge behind Notre Dame first so she could see its famous flying buttresses. Next, he zipped her up the undulating pavement that hugged the Louvre and Tuilieries. Knowing the bridges themselves were works of art, he downshifted so they could putter over Pont de l'Alma where big *bateaux mouches* were sleeping on beds of water, if not waterbeds.

Parker wanted Seabright to enjoy as many vantage points of the Seine's fantastic facades as possible, so he zigzagged across each of

Paris' 33 bridges at a variety of speeds. To cap off the metropolitan tour, he cruised to a stop at the Trocadero so that their approach to the Eiffel Tower would be as dramatic as the events of the night before, the details of which she had yet to divulge. Parker pointed his front fork at the gigantic candelabra, then his bike made a beeline for its web of steel until they were totally enveloped by its irregular shadows.

His niece seemed abnormally agitated by his choice for a *brioche* break, however, and insisted they end their excursion elsewhere since the Eiffel Tower had been the final destination for a different soul the night before. As well, she had a sneaking suspicion her uncle brought her back to the site of the murder just to elicit a response from her, if not a confession.

After removing the fullface guest helmet, Seabright pulled her hood over her head like the top on a convertible, raising Parker's suspicions to an all time high. "Why did you stop here of all places?" she griped, cradling the stars-and-stripes helmet like a patriotic bowling ball.

"I thought you'd like to see the Eiffel Tower. I didn't know if you'd seen it yet."

She drew the drawstring on her hood so tight that she looked like an alien. "I saw it every time we crossed the Seine, but I guess 33 sightings is not enough."

"You sound a wee bit defensive. Is there something you want to confess?"

"I confess I'm cold, which is why I'm going to put my helmet back on."

"You're going to climb the tower while wearing a fullface helmet?"

"I'm not climbing the stupid tower. Metal steps and clogs make for a bad marriage."

"How would you know?" He patted her on the back, but she stiffened like a corpse. "We have a saying here in France. *Qui s'excuse s'accuse,* to excuse yourself is to accuse yourself."

She raised the visor to talk as if safely tucked away inside a suit of armor. "I prefer the French phrases Robespierre is teaching me, like *Ecrasez L'infame!* Crush the church! Volcanic Voltaire put that cool logo on his letters."

Parker strapped on his half helmet, making sure she noticed the hellish orange flames that licked the skid lid. "Robespierre has a nasty attitude about the pew population for a priest."

"He's just exposing me to the errors in Christianity so that I can better defend it. Did you know Voltaire believed religion was made only to deceive stupid people?"

"Sin deceives both smart and stupid people. People who think they're smart do the dumbest things. Spend some time in Italy and you'll hear them say, Learned fools are the biggest fools. Deception is a party Satan throws for fools."

"How do you know? Did you save the party blower?" She mounted his metal stallion as if starring in her own rodeo, but she had to hold her horses until her uncle saddled up. Parker let his panhead purr for a minute, then they both bid Happy Trails to the scenic crime scene.

After a few loops around the Latin Quarter, her uncle cruised up Rue Valentin which prompted Seabright to knock on his helmet. She then motioned for him to pull over. Obeying with a measure of displeasure, he rolled to a stop near a crappy little *crepe* shop. Hoodless and helmetless, she danced around with unbridled curiosity as if she had just found her yellow brick road, at the end of which was a French wizard.

Knowing he wouldn't see her for a few days, Parker caught up with her to warn her about the caustic cleric. "Be careful when this guy starts quoting French writers, because not only did they author some of the best Christian literature, they also authored some of the most venomous attacks against it. Voltaire's dying words were 'I shall go to hell,' yet he brazenly declared that in 50 years the world would not hear of the Bible. 50 years later the British Museum paid half a million for one Bible at the same time that his book sold for pennies in Paris."

She peeked in a café window. "I'm not willing to miss out on the fun I plan to commit."

"I've come to realize I'm always going to miss somebody or something."

"You?" She glanced inside another café as if shopping for a certain customer.

"*Ja oui.* I'm a sentimental sap. When some of my dreams died, some of me died too."

"That's why I refuse to wake up from this dream until it's morning, *late* morning." A kiosk scored her one cold Kronenburg. "I'd rather be a fool for love than a fool for life."

"There's no need to be a fool for either. That's the fallacy of false dilemma again."

"My only dilemma is whether I should meet my priest for drinks before dinner or after."

The Bavarian barrister smiled with a patience painfully bought. "Been there, done that."

"Thanks for not telling me I couldn't possibly be in love with a man I just met."

"I know it's not only possible, it's highly probable," replied the seasoned biker. "Love is a state of mind, and you crossed that state line when your jet touched down in Europe."

She wound her hair around her finger like cotton candy on a stick. "Robert Louis Stevenson said love is an illogical adventure, but this can't get too crazy since he's a priest."

"So, what you're looking for is something like a controlled skid?"

"*Oui, oui!*"

"There's no such thing as a controlled skid."

"Whatever. Europe is good for experimenting since nobody knows me over here."

"Experimenting with what? Sin? God says your sin will find you out. Sin is expensive."

"Some things are worth the price. I don't fear a sail into the wrong port as much as I fear rotting away in a rocking chair of regret. I'm willing to trade a few mistakes for an adventure."

"I made a ministry out of my mistakes. Skip the pain and learn from my booboos."

"I look forward to making my own, but thanks for the offer." The Eiffel Tower loomed over the mansard roofs as if it were stalking her. "They say experience is the best teacher."

"It's the cruelest, that's for sure." Unflappable Parker suddenly looked a little flappy around the edges. "I know a pastor who watched one porno flick, and it changed his whole life."

"For the better, no doubt," she mumbled, loving the French names on the awnings.

"No, he lost his children, his church, and his chance at happiness."

"What about his wife?"

"I wanted to lose her." Parker turned a sheepish shade of chartreuse.

"When I look back, I doubt I'll regret things I've done, just things I failed to do."

"That's a perilous premise for Paris. Paris can seduce you in ways you'd never imagine."

"I doubt that. I have a very vivid imagination." She sank the brew, not admitting it tasted as tinny as the can it came in. "I feel like the mistress in *The French Lieutenant's Woman*. She said she drank wine, but it did not intoxicate her. Rather, it helped her see more clearly."

"No, it made her see less clearly—that's why she drank it. Who wants to see clearly if you are clearly having an affair? You need all the denial you can drink. You're into literature, so you should appreciate Shakespeare's advice: 'Gaze where you should, and that will clear your sight.'"

"How do you know so many quotes? My priest would be impressed by your collection."

"Some people frequent bars, I frequent beliefs. When something I read kicks me in the gluteus part of my maximus, I write it down on a Rolodex card, so I can revisit it later."

"I'm revisiting Scripture with Robespierre. He's helping me see things I never saw."

"I hope he isn't helping you see things that aren't there, Danielle...I mean, Seabright."

She talked as she walked backwards. "If I'm wrong, I'll just turn around down the road."

"It won't seem wrong down the road. Twain warned: it's easier to stay out than get out."

She glanced inside another pub, knowing her priest began refueling early. "Robespierre wouldn't even talk to you. He refuses to talk to people who tell him he's going to hell."

"Why do people think he's going to hell? Dingding. Maybe he's going to hell?"

"Like Nietzsche, he has a different take on what the Church should look like."

"His take might take you for a ride. The only thing new in theology is error. Nietzsche was so bloated with deception he boasted, 'There is no devil and no hell. Fear, therefore, nothing any more.' A priest who loves Nietzsche is not a priest from whom I would take communion."

"If loving him is wrong, maybe I don't need to be right right now."

"You're down the road," Parker lamented. "What other authors does he quote?"

"Rousseau. He personifies the French Enlightenment. His feelings *were* his faith."

"The proof of Rousseau's prodigal pudding is that he abandoned all five of his babies."

She searched for another Kronenburg kiosk. "Rousseau read the Bible every night."

"No, he read *into* the Bible every night. That's eisegesis, not exegesis."

She wished her uncle lived in Peru, not Paris. "We can disagree and both be right with God."

"Not if one of us is disagreeing with God. Don't obfuscate the obvious to accommodate the erroneous. When you deceive yourself, you become your own worst enemy."

He looked whimsically handsome in his Bavarian bikerwear, but she refused to tell him if he refused to play along with her plans. "I've always had a desire for forbidden love, if love really can be forbidden. God made me this way, so He can't damn me for who I love."

"Your Robespierre poached that premise from Homer. However, the fact that you want to do something doesn't justify your doing it. I pray Europe helps you sort out your convictions."

I just pray I'm not convicted of murder while in Europe, she mumbled to herself. "If I find myself in a jam, I'm sure Robespierre will help me get out of it."

"I'm sure he'll help you into a few, too. Let me help you."

She hesitated a moment, terrified of her honesty. "No, we love those we help…"

"Did you know Robespierre was a revolutionary who incited rebellion, individualism, and the guillotine but was thereafter guillotined by those same rebellious individuals he incited?"

"So?"

"So, this guy calls himself Robespierre for a reason."

"Yeah, it's his name." She couldn't wait to see the rest of Paris with her libertine friend.

Parker handed her a laminated business card that asked the bearer to do business with God. Disappointed that it wasn't a museum pass, she carped, "What the devil is this?"

"A devil-stopper. I call them temptation termination cards. Each card addresses a different degree of dangerous desire. Level one warns, 'If you do not do well, sin is crouching at the door.' Genesis 4:7. Why don't you tuck one in your cape to help you fight the good fight?"

Her gelatin eyes grew white cold. "I don't feel like fighting any battles on vacation."

"The devil doesn't take a vacation."

"I know." She held out her hand as if accepting the tab for a snack at pricey Le Vivarois. "You put a quote from the court of Louis XIV on this card? Cool. I'm trying to learn French quotes fast. 'Those who give themselves to God are delivered from countless evils.'"

"That quote pulled me out of a tailspin that could've sent my tail spinning off the Eiffel."

"I don't plan on going anywhere near the Eiffel ever again." Her eyes blinked nervously as she scanned the next verse on the card, Matthew 5:30. "Jesus said it's better to cut off anything that leads to sin rather than be cast into hell because of it? Look, I don't plan to party and fool around forever, but I deserve to have a good time after being good for so long."

Parker didn't point out the guilt and fear implicit in her response. Instead he bought her a baguette to get her to eat something, knowing where she was headed if she didn't. "You skipped Hosea 4:11. 'Wine and new wine take away the heart and spiritual understanding.'"

"I skipped it because I don't have a problem with drinking."

"I know. I skipped it when I didn't have a problem, either," he laughed. "Ezekiel 20:7 fixed my feet: 'Each one of you must reject those *horrors* which attract you.'"

Eager to star in a horror flick of her own, she looked for her priest in another pub window. "You put Shakespeare on this card, too? I lovvvvve Shakespeare. 'The prince of darkness is a gentleman.' I suppose that warning is a jab at Robespierre?"

"I didn't know Robespierre when I printed up these laminated cards."

"You're too black and white. Robespierre is helping me appreciate life's sophisticated shades of gray." She turned the card over disgustedly, wishing he would look away, so she could poach a postcard of the wines of Paris. "Why is there a conflagration on the flip side?"

"I printed a flaming inferno on the flip side with a ladder sticking out of it to remind us that God promised to provide us a way of escape out of every temptation. I Corinthians 10:13."

"Temptation is the last frontier."

"You don't honestly believe that."

"No, but Robespierre honestly believes that. I honestly believe I'll have another drink."

Parker's eyes gravitated to the looming landmark of steel. "I'm more concerned about this minister than the Eiffel Tower killer right now because the killer in our midst can only put an end to your life whereas a heretic can see to it that your agony only begins when this life ends."

CHAPTER FIVE

Montmartre Cemetery, Paris
1:27 p.m. 22 February

Like an open air museum of death just a few doors down from the porn pits of Pigalle, Montmartre Cemetery made the most of its eccentric city setting. Thousands of strange coffins had been "buried" above ground on a vast undulating field overshadowed by gnarly chestnut trees chockful of super-sized squirrels. Towering apartment buildings like Parker's overlooked the land of the dead like a stadium full of uninvited guests.

The nearly grassless graveyard stuffed to the gills with oddball burial vaults looked as if had been visited by a bulldozer that shoved the tombstones together to make room for more skeletal citizens once every century or so. The carrion kingdom played host to torsos frozen in marble, angels frozen in bronze, and half frozen cats frozen to the torsos, tombs, and angels. A modern blue bridge had sprawled its steel tentacles like a ceiling over an old section of necropolis plots, clearly demonstrating that some of the living no longer gave a rip about the dead, but most tourists kept their distance, afraid they might see evidence of a world elsewhere.

The ossuary orchard had been queerly terraced as if to bless some bodies with balcony views while burying others in a sod basement so as not to embarrass the Parisian public with their *mauvais gout.* Medieval signs outlined the brick lanes that crisscrossed the cemetery, and it was on a bench near one such sign that Robespierre met up with seduceable Seabright.

Whipping her hair around like a model in a shampoo shoot, Seabright was none too happy when her black tendrils knocked over their wine bottle. Casting her locks in the opposite direction, she cared less when they snagged on a cemetery urn. "Is Robespierre your real name?"

A spasm of irritation crossed his face as he poured the wine. "You ask this...why?"

"A friend of mine wanted to know, that's all."

The 17th century throwback threw back some wine as he tucked his tights in his knickers. "Is this someone I should be concerned about? A man competing for your affections, perhaps?"

She glanced up at Parker's apartment. "He is rather fond of me..."

"You are staying with this man, *oui*?"

"*Oui.* How did you know?"

"I could tell by the direction you entered the cemetery." He sniffed the wine as if the aroma itself were intoxicating. "The skeleton key in your pocket is also a clue to his residence."

"It isn't really a skeleton key, or were you making another mortuary pun?"

"A pun, perhaps." He stuck his tongue in the wine. "May I see the key, *s'il vous plait*?"

Balancing her glass carefully, she dug for the key, but her fingers ran into Parker's temptation termination card instead. Dodging the killjoy card, she fished out Parker's key. "The guy I'm staying with is my uncle, by the way, not my boyfriend."

"That is good news indeed. Is your brother also staying with you?"

"*Oui,* but both of them are gone during the day if you want to come over."

"I would like to meet him sometime."

"What a coincidence. Parker would like to meet you." She helped herself to more wine.

He stroked his mustache with great vexation of spirit, pressing down hard on it as if it were a glue-on. "It is your brother I wish to meet, not your uncle." Realizing his complexity frightened her, he smiled reassuringly as he opened his picnic basket. "I felt *pitie* for you because you try to write down my teachings, so I brought this machine that will record our conversations for you. Do copy the tape for me so I can hear the sound of your voice as I fall asleep."

"You bought this for me? How thoughtful of you!" She kissed him on the cheek as a hearse crept past with a dancing squirrel for a hood ornament. "I want to see all the sights of Paris with you, *sans* guilt. Wine will help, but when the wine wears off I have to *know* what's wrong with the Bible or I'll start feeling guilty all over again. I tried to explain your theology to Parker, but he said your new Christianity is no Christianity."

"'If we would destroy the Christian religion, we must first of all destroy man's belief in the Bible,' so said Voltaire. I'm trying to bring back the old religion, not a new Christianity."

Her eyebrows expressed alarm. "My professor called Satanism 'the old religion.'"

"*Sauve-qui-peut!* Run for your life!" he laughed, poking his pinkies through his pony tail like devil's horns. He reached into his picnic basket again and showered her lap with pebbles.

Seabright brushed off the pebbles as Robespierre walked around and placed pebbles on different shed-sized tombs. As if they had a life of their own, the cemetery's stone crosses seemed to grow larger and more pronounced as she stared at them. "Why don't you just start your own church, or whatever you'd call it since it wouldn't, technically, be Christian?"

"*Sacre bleu!* The true books of Christianity have been lost and suppressed."

"If they have been lost and suppressed, how do you know they ever existed?"

"I cannot produce as proof those parchments that have already been destroyed."

She tried to believe him. "So, the fact that they don't exist proves their existence?"

"*Coup d'autorite!* Your Bible is a *melange* of myths written by morons for morons."

"But Daniel, Solomon, Isaiah, Paul, Luke and other authors were highly educated."

"Not as highly educated as *moi*, but the Church turns a blind eye to my erudition."

"You make the Bible say what you want to hear, but they won't hear of it?" she teased.

"*Bouche cousue!* The wine, it brings out the beast in you, not the best in you." He squirmed like a caterpillar to pique her suspicions about him, knowing suspicion could serve as foreplay. "A Harvard scholar researched the *radotage* of apocryphal documents and found references to my Scripture interpretations on a fourth century text from preliterate Spain."

"If Spain was preliterate, it had no texts. Regardless, are these 'texts' your Bible?"

He smiled a smile that made mush of her. "No, my heart is my Bible. My mind is my Bible. I'll be damned if some provincial preacher is going to tell me how to live my life."

"You'll be damned if you don't, according to those provincial preachers."

He placed more pebbles on coffin lids. "My God is bigger than the Bible."

"Is your God the God of the Bible? Why are you putting pebbles on people's tombs?"

"I saw Jews doing this in Jerusalem. They put pebbles on giant sarcophagi."

"I prefer flowers."

"Then flowers I shall place on your tomb. As for the Bible, Edward Gibbon observed in *The Decline and Fall of the Roman Empire* that religion is an inevitable mixture of error and corruption that it contracted from its long residence on earth. Same goes for Scripture, *oui*?"

"But archaeology has confirmed most of the names, dates, and history in the Bible, and many of its prophecies have already been fulfilled," she shot back just to show off. "There were numerous eyewitnesses to the resurrection who died rather than recant their testimony."

"*Mademoiselle*, that was just a conspiracy to perpetuate their personal popularity."

"Dead disciples don't win popularity contests. Besides, nobody dies for a lie."

Robespierre balanced a pebble on her head. "Do not be so gullible, *cherie*."

"Gullible? That's the worst of all insults. Professor, I wish massive chunks of the Bible weren't true, but the fact that it tells me things I *don't* want to hear lends credence to its authenticity. Most people's religion sounds suspiciously like themselves."

Robespierre deposited his derriere on a blank tombstone then rubbed his hand across the smooth marble surface. "This is all that was 'written.' Man made up the rules, *mademoiselle*."

"But the Bible says Jesus came to fulfill the Law, not to abolish it."

"There you go again with the Bible. The Bible is your problem."

She stared into her wine. "If only there was a way to get around it..."

"Learn to think abstractly, then you can abstract what you want from it," he laughed, filling her glass to the brim. "A girl as bright and sunny as you must have a dark side..."

She smiled like Mona Lisa, letting him guess how dark it could get. "I'm enjoying this death park with a priest by my side to protect me from its poltergeists, but I hate to think what could've hatched inside that gargantuan green metal mausoleum to your right."

"It is a container for a fallen comrade, or perhaps a fallen angel." Robespierre fished his Englishman's stemwinder watch out of his pants. "When do I get to meet your family?"

Delighted that he was taking their friendship to the next level, she swooned to the extent possible while reclining, wanting to melt like butter in his arms. Her heart sank, however, when she noticed a ring on his finger. Honing in on the initials etched into its shiny surface, she replied, "My hometown is Harborpoint, but Paris is already beginning to feel like home to me."

Her nosiness did not escape his attention. "This is my sister's class ring," he explained with a wry smile. "She died in a rollerblading accident last year."

"You rollerblade in Paris?"

"Right down Boulevard Saint Germain every Saturday night, love. It's a 30 kilometre skate across town. My dear sis slid under a lorry when it turned right on Boul'Mich."

"Is a lorry one of those glorified go-carts that Parisians park two to a parking space?"

"No, a lorry is a mini-truck with a boxy back end. It's a British term, actually. Never mind my sister's misfortunes, it is your brother I wish to meet. His name is James, right?"

"Right." Her face flinched with confusion. "Why do you want to meet him?"

"*S'il vous plait*, I want to help him. I shall explain later." He waved his hand in a circle. "Montmartre Cemetery is not just any village of the damned. Artistic luminaries live here."

"But I have not yet seen the artists of Montmartre up on Place du Tertre."

"I shall transport you there, but I have friends to visit here first."

"Hence, the pebbles, I presume." Unaccustomed to the attention of an older man, she tried to think of something sophisticated to say, wishing she could draw from Parker's quiver of quotes. "You're a man of God, so you can show me all the ways in which God is art."

"*Avec plaisir!* Nothing teaches you to color outside the lines faster than a visit to *sans frein* Montmartre." He drew his hair over his shoulder like a Southern Belle. "I wished not to take you to the tourist haunts *tout de suite* lest you think me an impostor."

"An impostor? Do you not possess what you profess?" she laughed.

"*Je ne comprends pas*. Is that some sort of Jesus *je ne sais quoi*?"

"No, that's what our professors asked us at Civitas Dei during bouts of backsliding."

"Civitas Dei?"

"College. My folks insisted on inculcating James and me with a Christian education."

"*You* are a Christian?" he chuckled, uncorking another bottle.

"More or less. Like Augustine, I want to be well versed in both pagan and pious literature since I figure one will either enhance or undermine the other."

"You are open to either eventuality?" he whispered like a vulture ventriloquist.

"I'll follow your lead. Didn't France say if the path is pretty, don't ask where it leads?"

"*Oui*, create your own path, your own reality. Heaven and hell are mere figments of our collective imagination. The Bible is not God, so it needs to be corrected by men like me."

"'We have corrected Thy work'? That's what the fool said to Christ in the greatest novel ever written, Dostoyevsky's *Brothers Karamazov.*" She searched for a cemetery souvenir but stopped short of robbing a grave. "No correction tape works on the Bible."

"Ignorance is bliss, is it not?"

She chuckled, enjoying the feisty exchange. "Do women call you Father Robespierre?"

"No. *Pere* is 'father' in French, but I hope you don't think of me as your father."

"Of course not," she cooed. Her face flooded red with sexual shyness. "You said you're also a professor at the Sorbonne. What is it you profess?"

"*Faux devot* and *faux bonhomme.*" He bowed like a matador who liked shooting the bull instead of fighting bulls. "You probably wonder why I speak English so well."

"Do you teach English as a second language?"

"How did you guess, *amie de coeur*? I also teach a course on English Literature."

"I'm literary like the Left Bank, too. I'm mad about monikers, are you?"

"*Certainement.*" The pastor primped his cufflinks. "Has your brother a pseudonym?"

"Two. Walking Wallpaper and Tame James. Do you like to make sport of words?"

"*Oui*, I like to play games, but I play for keeps." Robespierre held two fingers up behind his ears as if they were elf's appendages. "I fear we shall get on famously."

"One minute you sound French, the next you sound British. You Europeans are *tres* cosmopolitan." Seabright stole another glance at Parker's apartment.

"Who are you looking for? Are you trying to signal someone?"

"Yes, the mothership," she laughed while chucking a chestnut at a statue's manhood.

"Your eyes shifted to the left, so I know you're lying."

"Okay, my favorite Martian asked if you could speak up because the audio is being garbled by the gravestones." Seabright jumped on to the brick lane when a cat lunged out of a tomb like a diminutive dybbuk, hoping to catch a ride across town to the tomb of a friend on a Compagnie de Marbreries truck. "I understand the British influence in your inflections since the Chunnel puts Britain in your backyard, but how do you know so much American slang?"

"Hollywood is here and here below. The Metro is the poor man's museum. It houses Hollywood posters and Louvre pieces. I played an American in many a melodramatic role."

"I hate to break it to you, but Americans don't wear floral diadems, leggings, and eyebrow rings. Speaking of clothes, Uncle Parker asked me if you wear a cross. I told him you did."

"You're a liar *and* a thief, two qualities I admire in a woman."

Her face contorted itself with unconfessed sin. "I assumed you wear your priesthood inside that Bohemian uniform," Seabright laughed. "What makes you think I'm a thief?"

"I was at the Eiffel when you were at the Eiffel."

Her cheeks grew hot as a griddle. "I didn't swipe anything at the Eiffel."

"*A vrai dire.* Indeed, you stole that *boules* ball at Parc Chien en route to the Eiffel." He withheld the wine until the shock set in. "I saw in you intense *animus furandi.*"

She couldn't believe he had been watching her every move. "Passion?"

"No, I saw in you the zeal to steal." He splashed her glass with a tease of wine.

Shifting her body away from him self-protectively, she quaffed the *vin mousseux* to extinguish the guilt she could not expiate. "Did you follow me to the Eiffel to get me to confess?"

Robespierre laughed out loud. "I thought you were following *me* to get *me* to confess."

"To what? Not saying enough Hail Marys while hungering for a woman?"

He pressed his leg to hers. "You are sexually frustrated, *cherie*."

"Takes one to know one." She uncrossed her legs, letting herself enjoy the danger.

"I gather you stumbled into my happy hunting ground for a reason."

"You're deliciously droll, but Parker thinks the devil is using you to undermine my faith so that I'll be easy prey for the Eiffel Tower killer."

"There is a killer on the loose in Paris?"

"Yes. Someone was killed up on the Eiffel Tower last night."

"How much of this killing did you see?"

"Nothing, believe me."

"I do believe you because you said the victim was killed *up* on the Eiffel Tower." He refilled her glass. "*Au contraire,* the newspapers report that a man died underneath it."

"Did you see anything?"

"I saw plenty." He chewed on his lower lip, trapping a hair that had broken loose from his broom mustache. "The authorities needed a collar to say last rites at the *accidente,* so they collared me." He fired the wine cork into the dark recesses of a gated tomb as his eyes roved across the apartment windows which surrounded them.

"Why are you referring to it as an *accidente*? It wasn't a suicide or murder?"

"You seem to want it to be a suicide or a murder. That's *tres* telling. I take a keen interest in criminal behavior, especially yours." He looped his headband around her wrists like handcuffs and drew her towards him. "How long have you been stealing, Danielle?"

Wine toppled out of her glass. Her eyes traveled back to Parker's place as she tried to keep her drug of choice from spilling on a coffin lid. "If I have to confess it might as well be to a priest. For as long as I can remember, that's how long I've been borrowing things."

"Is the risk your reward? Do you want to be punished so you'll know God exists?"

"Those are good questions. Unfortunately, I don't have any good answers."

He dipped his finger in the wine then made the sign of the cross on her forehead. "I absolve you of your sins." He let her drink from the bottle as if it were part of the ritual. "Now it's my turn to confess: I confess it's fun watching unconfessed sin snowball into a life of crime."

Her smile capsized. "I wouldn't exactly call it a life of crime."

"Of course you wouldn't, that's why I did. No one calls it crime until he's done time. My years of experience in hand-carved confessionals can teach you this: unforgiveness is a spigot for serial sin. Mistaking bitterness for balm is like mistaking a bidet for a drinking fountain."

Agitated but fascinated, she felt her trust crossing over into love. She imagined how scared she would feel in the graveyard at night without him. "The books people read tell me a lot about them. I know you're not a fan of the Bible, but what authors do you like, professor?"

"I rather enjoy the Enlightenment authors, I can tell you. They took a fancy to pleasure, especially sexual pleasure. Their motto is mine: Question Authority. They throw the furniture of theology about a bit, but there's nothing quite like a spot of anarchy to cheer one up."

"Now you sound like a Brit again. Is that because England once occupied France?"

"I always sound a bit Brit when I commune with the spirits. Don't ask me why."

"Don't ask you why you commune with spirits or don't ask you why you sound British?"

"I shouldn't worry your pretty little head about either, mate."

She scuffed at the dirt like a nervous batter. "Do you wish you had a mate?"

"Theoretically, I am married to God."

A pallor spread across her face like a burial shroud. "Theoretically? Do you mean to tell me you've already broken your vows?" she asked with a jealous tenor.

He smoothed out his pantyhose. "It's hard to break something you don't believe in."

"*Tres* true." She liked the level at which the liaison was proceeding and didn't see any need to sabotage it. "What literature do you recommend, professor?"

"Diderot is good reading." He tightened the clip on his ponytail. "'Men will never be free until the last king is strangled with the entrails of the last priest.' That is Diderot."

Seabright choked on her surprise. "That's a strange thing for a priest to say."

"All the more reason to say it!" He clinked his glass to hers. "Voltaire said orthodox Christianity was mankind's worst enemy. It still is. There was nothing Christian about Jesus."

"There wasn't?"

"Jesus was not a Christian. Christianity is a gross misrepresentation of Jesus's life."

"Maybe you *are* the Big, Bad Wolf." She leaned toward him with an iniquitous inquisitiveness. "However, there are aspects of Christianity I could do without, celibacy and sobriety for starters. I'd give anything to be able to live it up and not go down when I die," she laughed, assuming her grave would not be dug for many years.

"Then I shall share with you the true papyrus texts like the Gospel of Mary, the Gospel of Thomas and the Gospel to the Egyptians, favorites of misunderstood scholars."

"Apostates always claim to be misunderstood," she provoked him.

After a gulp of gusto, Robespierre felt fully adrenalized to startle her desires. "I take the cross seriously. Even if something I do is a sin, it is as if it never happened. *Damnant quod non intelligunt.* To understand all is to forgive all. God understands all, ergo, God forgives all."

"Wow, someone could use that kind of logic as a license to kill."

"Jesus died for our sins, so why not honor Him by committing sins worthy of death?"

"Logic like that could get us both killed," she laughed.

"*Vogue la galere!*" He tossed some grave flowers in the air like fragrant fireworks.

"But Jesus never abrogated the sexual code. If anything, he made it less liberal."

"The definition of sexuality will change, as will the definition of sin. Why deprive yourself? Buddha fasted until his hair fell out, and it didn't earn him Enlightenment."

The chalky apartments topped with gray mansard roofs looked eerily reminiscent of the chalky mausoleums topped with gray lids that surrounded her. "Buddha was no Jesus. I heard the Buddhist monks' monotone drones being broadcast across the temple grounds in bang-a-gong Hong Kong, and my hair stood on end. It was sorcery and a side of rice, like camping out with a cult of zombies. The evil in the air was palpable. Besides, Buddha was agnostic about whether or not God even exists, so I wouldn't put his number on my speed dial for spiritual advice."

"Voltaire was also agnostic, *mademoiselle*. He said, 'If God did not exist, it would be necessary to invent him.' Ergo, why believe in God if God does not exist?"

"You can't possibly be a priest. Parker warned me about your undermining my faith."

"You have no faith or you would not be talking to me."

She hated what age did to arrogant men and resolved never to have a sex change. As the alcohol began to kick in, she cozied up to a tombstone, finding the cold stone strangely soothing. "Unbelief is equated with wickedness in the Bible, so your doubt could damn you to hell."

"I doubt that," he laughed, licking his lips. "Doubt is the fountain of youth."

"Being negative does not have a positive effect on your life." She pitched a chestnut into a stone basin, but it felt as if something wanted to pitch it back at her.

He twisted his ring so hard it looked as if he were trying to detach his finger. This having failed, he drew her eyelids closed. "*Cherie*, it is a sin the way people use Scripture."

She rolled over on the coffin, toes up. "*Au contraire,* my legal eagle uncle taught me the Latin phrase *abusus non tollit usum dictum.* The abuse of a book does not invalidate the book."

He poured wine into each letter on the headstone. "I serve a God that is living, not the words on a printed page. My heroes are outside of mainstream Christianity, brave men who reinterpreted Scripture in a way that celebrates the diversity of our alleged abominations."

"That's not just outside the mainstream, that's outside of any stream."

He smiled, clearly enjoying himself. "We're digging our own stream, brewing our own living water. Granted, a certain level of intoxication is a *sine qua non* for our celebrations."

She wished he wouldn't waste the wine. "I know my enlightenment is contingent upon embracing foreign concepts," she hedged while sniffing a funerary flower, "but your theology sounds as artificial as these plastic petals," she goaded him, thinking he needed a good goad.

"*Sacre bleu!* Foreign tastes are not fast foods; they take time to acquire. The mind expels new ideas the way the body expels new medicines, but you know medicines are good for you."

"You beg the question when you equate antibiblical notions with medicines." She slapped her cheek. "Sorry, that's my uncle talking. Sometimes I'm an unwitting channel for his logic."

"Perhaps your spirituality is not so different from mine. I channel, too."

"No you don't. That's necromancy, another abomination. You sure love to shock people." Her head was spinning, but she didn't want to do anything to stop it from spinning.

"I like to make people think. We must dismantle the supercastles of the superstitious."

"I can't say as I agree with all of your positions. Then again, I can't say as I agree with all of mine," she giggled, determined to beg, borrow or steal more wine.

Robespierre panned the cemetery, knowing he held her eyes with his. "*Cherie*, each mausoleum is like a miniature prison, and Jesus told us to visit the prisoners."

"Not dead prisoners." She pulled away like a baby from a bearded man in a red suit.

"Voltaire would disagree. He believed organized religion is tyranny. He said: 'Animals have this advantage over man: they have no theologians to instruct them.'"

Seabright felt as if she had been sedated for surgery, but she didn't want to sleep the sleep of death when she was just beginning to live her life. She swirled her wine coyly. "Don't you think the fact that Voltaire had a mistress could have prejudiced his opinion against Christianity?"

He stiffened like a corpse. "*Sacre bleu!* Even if the Bible is inspired, does that mean only the Bible is inspired? Maybe witchcraft is inspired differently for witches." Robespierre remained as calm as a cadaver when a cat leapt out of a burial chamber like a jack in the box. "I shall leave my picnic basket to comfort some grieving grandmother, but my spiritual reading tells me I must leave before God and every other soul topped full of vengeance gets his knickers in a twist." He puckered like a carp. "I shall transport your heart to Montmartre on a fun *funiculare* now. Trust me, I'll levitate your understanding to new destinations."

"I naturally trust you, you're a priest. Besides, I'd be traipsing through the courts of the French kings with my boring brother if adventure weren't on my agenda. We're *tres simpatico, pere*." She let herself tumble into the dark pool of his eyes, certain the fall was worth the trip.

"*Vogue la galere!* Live a fearless life, for a cowardly life is a premature death."

"That's Tame James for you. He's enigmatic, emotionally vacant, and fickle."

Robespierre flicked the tassels on his headband back and forth, although the totality of his hair seemed to move with it. "Where did your pretty brother pop off to today?"

"Some stupid historical site. He's been very sneaky lately. It's not like him."

"Is it like you?" he baited her.

"It could be," she replied, resolved that her shyness would not keep her at home any more.

"If you are afraid of me, you can bring your brother with you next time."

"Why would I be afraid?" she laughed, growing more comfortable with the coffins.

"One never knows." He arched his eyebrows with a delicious gesture of ill intent as he led her out of the shadowy cemetery to colorful Rue Caulaincourt.

CHAPTER SIX

Poste de Police, Eiffel Tower
3:43 p.m. 22 February

The *commissariat's* resident curmudgeon primped his tangle of whitish hair that looked like a snarl of used dental floss. He then interrogated his own officer as if it were a crime just to be in one's prime. "Which Civitas Dei students recently purchased passports to Paris? Was it not the woman in cape and clogs that our cameras saw on the Eiffel Tower the night of the murder?"

The junior cop twisted his badge nervously, not wanting to rat the girl out but not wanting to jeopardize his job, either. "Yes, she was one of two. I ran a cross-check on the names of Civitas Dei students, the names on passengers' lists, and the names on credit card receipts from the tower the night of the murder. Her college faxed this photograph to me. Americans call it a yearbook photo. The image bears some resemblance to the girl in our security films."

"What is her name?"

"Danielle Seabright."

"We now have proof that the fake suicide note was written on her Civitas Dei College stationery, the pen that was thrust into the victim's leg was also from Civitas Dei, she was photographed at the scene of the murder, and she is a thief three times over. Find her."

"But the fact that Danielle Seabright went to Civitas Dei should exonerate her. No college educated woman would be so dumb as to implicate herself with her school's pen and paper."

The old officer picked his nose with a pipe cleaner. "She was drinking. One does dumb things when one drinks."

The young cop couldn't argue with his assertion, remembering how he had auditioned for the Folies Bergere on a night when they weren't taking auditions after an evening of pubbing in Paris. "How can you ignore the fact that another Civitas Dei student purchased a passport to Paris recently? Remember the photo found in the victim's wallet? The guy pictured with the girl was her brother, James Woodlawn Seabright, not some evil accomplice."

"Family members make the best accomplices."

"I think we should be questioning that gypsy tattler who paid our cop shop a visit."

"There is no Bohemian gypsy tattler on the security films."

He wondered if the old chauvinist suspected all women. "Did you find a kill bag?"

"No. You checked out the Chunnel link. Did they find a kill bag in England?"

"No, just the killer's tracks. If he didn't love wine, we wouldn't even have tracks."

"Did you get a description of this serial slayer haunting the English countryside?"

"A catalog of descriptions. He changes clothes more often than a runway model."

"Then how do you know one man is responsible for all the murders?"

"He brags, of course. Evil always brags. He wants us bumbling detectives to know he pulled it off again. His type often like to watch the investigation from a safe distance."

"There is no safe distance." Grumpy smiled, enjoying the evil resident inside himself.

CHAPTER SEVEN

Place du Tertre, Montmartre
5:07 p.m. 22 February

In a picturesque square nestled inside winding brick lanes, artists painted what their hearts felt, uncertain whether the browsing public would embrace their efforts. The fortunate ones did not care. Bright red umbrellas sprouted occasionally like fairy tale mushrooms to protect the canvases from the spitting rain. International onlookers sat close by in café chairs, drinking in each moment of creation while sipping steaming javas. The artists recorded Montmartre's village charm with more warmth and color than harsh, cold reality since they knew happy memories were all that the tourists wanted to keep alive in their hearts when they hung their paintings on the dead walls of their suffocating cubicles in less scenic pieces of real estate on the planet.

Gray mansard roofs, clay pot chimneys, Old World lanterns, crayon-colored awnings, and cheerful flowerboxes decorated medieval Montmartre while tortuous cobble lanes arrested the frenetic pace which infected Paris proper 430 feet below the artists' colony. No matter which serpentine route Seabright chose, the ice cream domes of Sacre Coeur kept popping into view.

"Renoir, Manet, Degas, and Dali strolled these streets, giving birth to visual poems which eulogized their pain," Robespierre explained as Seabright passed one of the few windmills left on the butte, although it looked more like a wooden outhouse than a wind machine.

"Nature is God's canvas writ large, isn't it," she speculated, happy to find herself capable of speculating. "But you said art has no laws, and you also said God is art, so God is lawless?"

"You are a fast learner. Now abandon yourself to all that is art, to all that is lawlessness."

"Art does transport me into the Eternal. Art must be a glimpse into God's heart."

"And the devil's. But the devil is better at music than art. It's hard to corrupt a lad with a good painting, not that I haven't tried." He glanced inside a varnished wood cheese shop dressed with a dark java interior. Never mind the fifty flavors of *fromage,* he wanted the wine that went with it. "God is more like the devil than you think. The Church turned that truth upside down."

"The Bible says life on earth is kind of mysterious like a dark mirror, but dark isn't upside down. Maybe you're the one who's upside down," she teased while pretending to flip him.

He bent over to look up at her through his legs. "Speaking of mirrors, David put mirrors in front of his huge paintings inside the Louvre so that you can see yourself in his paintings."

"I love art. I'm so literary, and it's so not. Art says stuff that can't be put into words." She stopped when her eyes fell on the famous Café Le Consulat's candy-striped awning. "Parker said the paint is so deep on the D'Orsay Van Goghs they look 3-D like framed sculpture."

"Van Gogh lived a wonderrrrrrfully disturbbbbbbed life, didn't he. His father was a minister, and Van Gogh himself was a minister to miners, so his tortured works are riddled with religious symbolism. Bouts of madness, self-mutilation, and self-murder naturally followed."

"My uncle would call that a causal fallacy." She showed him the list of Latin terms Parker copied for her, knowing she was eager to learn foreign phrases. "*Post hoc ergo propter hoc,* after this therefore because of this. You indulge in an invalid conclusion when you assume that Van Gogh's preaching derailed him. He bowed to Buddha before he blew himself away, so maybe that derailed him. The Bible warns that some who preach the gospel will be cast away."

"Your uncle's influence is underrated." The gypsy walked backwards to see if she would follow. "Paint the art that is in your heart—this will reveal your yellow brick road. No sin is as self-righteous as self-repression. Van Gogh shot himself, and Cezanne kept skulls in his studio."

"Therefore what?" Seabright laughed, too smart to be unsuspecting.

"God is art, but art can make you sick."

"*Ignoratio elenchi* and *non sequitur*. Your conclusion does not follow from your premises," she said with precocious intensity as a mime asked her for a handout with his hands.

"*Semper ubi sub ubi!* Don't forget to wear underwear!" Robespierre joked.

"Don't you think Van Gogh's pain could've had something to do with the fact that he only sold one painting even though he painted something like 900? Pain was his only patron. His last work, that wheatfield and crows thing, vividly captures his torment, but his torment was only beginning when he died at age 37 if he went to hell. Van Gogh's apostasy probably cursed his creations, not to mention his soul."

"I like it when a student puts up a fight. It makes the game more interesting." He waltzed into a gallery of Monets and Seurats, the paint on which was still wet. "When students asked Buddha for a Bible, he gave them a blank scroll, saying, 'These are the true Scriptures.'"

"That's because Buddha was in the dark about whether or not God even exists. I ain't no naif, professor. If you want to destroy my faith, you'll have to do better than that."

"I am only testing your faith the way a professor tests his star pupil. Seat yourself in my classroom of the future." He brushed the top of her hand with his mustache. "Nietzsche said what is done out of love takes place beyond the categories of good and evil."

"I can live with that. Maybe Nietzsche isn't public enemy number one after all."

He bowed like an actor without a stage. "I'm glad to see these lights turning on for you."

"But count me out of your control groups, because I refuse to be controlled by anyone."

"Then there is hope for you after all." The free thinker crowned her with his gypsy diadem then spun her toward a rack of barroom ballerina posters. "Not every artist drinks himself to death after coming unglued upstairs from doing unnatural things downstairs. Toulouse-Lautrec could barely walk yet he managed to capture the art of dance in color-splashed posters that celebrate the dark side of life, and the dark side of ourselves."

"Why glamorize darkness?" she asked, thinking his broads were a bit broad in the beam.

"Perhaps you shall be more trouble than you are worth, my pretty."

"Did I take a wrong turn on to Damnation Boulevard and don't even know it?"

"What you don't know can't hurt you." He curtsied like a father who thought himself a mother. Stepping under a red awning, he led her into a fun little shop to show her masterpieces that had been printed on pillboxes, potholders, placemats, pens, pajamas and postpartum pottery.

"Art is the currency of the brave new world I wish to conquer," she cooed.

Upon leaving the shop, Robespierre knelt down on his knickers and deposited a wad of cash in a beggar's hands, enough to keep his electric cello in business until his tax refund came in, or his tax forms were sent out, whichever came first. "Life on Montmartre is as pricey as Parisian snails," he explained, making the sign of the cross with his whole body. "I have learned to be sentient to all souls, living and dead, by holding out my hands to receive the black stigmata."

Her face looked as flabbergasted as a Trick-or-Treater who got fruit instead of candy. "I don't want any more death in my life. Ever since I came to Paris I've been having this recurring nightmare where I die in a plane crash. Death scares me almost as much as my life right now."

"Then by all means, do not let me kill you." Another Montmartre caricaturist tried to make a client out of him. "What is the source of these guilt feelings, Little Red Riding Hood?"

"Guilt feelings?"

"Death dreams are the reflecting pond of a guilty conscience."

"They only reflect the fear and negativity my uncle instilled in me when he gave me this stupid temptation termination card. Never underestimate the power of suggestion."

"I never do. I suggest you confess your sins so you can put some life back in your life."

She glanced at the street painter's rendition of Robespierre. His mouthy caricature made him look like a Bohemian Bugs Bunny. "*Pere*, I know I'm going out on a limb, but..."

"That's where you fully intended to go the moment you started drinking."

"Guilty as charged." She kicked at the cobblestones. "Tennessee Williams said devils can be driven out of the heart by the touch of a hand on a hand, or a mouth on a mouth…"

"*Certainement.* God is closest to the surface of our skin. When we touch each other, God flows through us. She speaks softly through the canvas of our flesh."

"She? I like that. I bet you really miss women…touching them, I mean."

He painted his mouth shut with his hand. "Like you Yanks, I'll take the Fifth."

"You wouldn't take the Fifth after drinking a fifth. Nothing loosens the tongue like toxins. Nothing unleashes temptations like toxins, either, according to Parker."

"Ah, yes. The Gospel According to Parker. And he is a missionary to my country? Then I am glad Buddhists are being sent to your country. I hate theological imperialism."

"Oh, it isn't theological imperialism when Buddhists do it? Let's be honest and admit the fact that isn't theological imperialism at all if the Bible is true. Deception damns souls."

He drew Tolstoy from his quote tote: "'It would be good if everything were as clear and simple as it seems to Princess Marya.' This blost world is dreadfully higgledy-piggledy."

"Now you sound so British again. Do you like Brit wits like Bronte?"

"Rah-thar! I shouldn't wonder that you'd fancy an English tea via the Chunnel, love!"

"I'd love a visit, and I love that you call me 'love.' It's playful and daring like us. I feel so dreadfully alive and dreadfully happy that I want to pick up a brush and paint something new and bright and colorful with no darkness in it at all. Do you go to England often?"

"It's a home away from home, and it sure aint Omaha," Robespierre replied.

"Where *is* home?" she asked, hoping it might be her home someday, too.

His eyes panned Montmartre's delicate black balconies before coming to rest on her sunny green eyes. "Home is where hope resides, and I see a horizon of hope in your eyes. Your face is like a bird's, clean and natural with striking features, but it has not been cuddled and kissed enough like a puppy's face. There is no anesthetic for grief like the hope I see in your eyes."

"What is it you're grieving?" she asked, competitive about his affections.

"The loss of life in my life." He maintained a certain distance, a distance she didn't understand. She wanted him to lace his fingers through hers as they entered Place du Tertre, but she knew a romance that was taboo would come with a good helping of torment. Staking his claim at an outdoor table, he pulled out a wooden café chair for her, postponing the torment.

She wasted no time flagging down the *garcon* for a carafe. Next, she borrowed a pack of unattended smokes with childlike glee, but she gasped for air as her lungs filled with smoke.

"Have you something to confess?" he asked, eyeing her with amusement.

"Would I be burning my breathing bags if I didn't?" She crossed her eyes to make a kaleidoscope out of the Christmas lights that no one had bothered to take down.

"You can be honest with me." The priest returned the smokes to the cancer patient.

She felt both comfortable and uncomfortable with him, needing his fatherly advice but not wanting to scare him off by saying something a father couldn't forget. "I think it was my Civitas Dei pen that ended up in the leg of that dead guy under the Eiffel Tower the other night."

He combed his mustache with his teeth. "Were you drinking at the time?"

"With any luck I was."

"Then you probably do not remember the episode clearly."

"Clear enough to know I didn't do it!" She realized it was more fun to watch smoke than inhale it. "How did my pen wind up in a corpse when I loaned it to a weirdo in wingtips?"

He made a face suitable for framing…with a noose. "What did this weirdo look like?"

"Satan in a suit. He was slick and debonair with slicked-back hair, tailor-made top to bottom. He was everything you aren't, and he had teeth like a train wreck."

He groaned with disbelief. "I have never seen a suit on the tower. Must I play along with this fanciful fabrication? You are framing your brother for someone *you* killed, right?"

"Wrong. I'd like to kill James at times, but I'm not talented enough to frame anybody."

"If I can be of any assistance…"

"You're so funny and not entirely stupid like most people." She squeezed his arm as if it were a life preserver. "I don't know what I'd do if I didn't have a man of God to talk to today."

"*Je comprends*." He leaned toward her. "Everything you say to me is confidential."

"My *boules* ball tumbled out of my cape when I sneaked up the Eiffel Tower, but it wasn't until I exited the elevator that I noticed a ball like mine near the victim."

Robespierre toyed with his eyebrow ring. "Tell me more, *s'il vous plait*."

"There's nothing more to tell."

"You saw nothing else?"

"No." She dabbed the sweat off her lip. "What should I do, father? I can't confide in the cops since I stole the stupid ball. Do you think my ball could still be wedged in the webbing?"

"No." He folded his hands in a visual prayer. "Your brother is involved in this debacle."

"How?" Fully attentive to any details that might exonerate her, she allowed the alcohol to awaken an anger already resident in her. "Was James at the tower that night, too?"

"*Oui.*" His face looked like an iceberg that was concealing some undisclosed danger below the surface. "I am sorry if this news upsets you, *cherie*."

She didn't want to admit that it didn't entirely upset her. "You better order another carafe if you want to keep the confessions coming." A bright yellow café umbrella tumbled on to an artist's easel while its lonely attendant nibbled a raspberry crepe at a nearby cafe, her hands raw from painting in the cold. "How do you know my brother was at the tower?"

"I recognized him from the picture you showed me. He did it with your *boules* ball."

Alarms went off in her mind. "James whacked the guy with the ball I borrowed?"

"It looked that way from my vantage point, and I had a very good vantage point."

"Were you on the tower?"

"*Oui.*"

She cradled the carafe as if it were her baby. "Why didn't you call the cops?"

"I knew it would be better for James to confess privately first. *De temps en temps,* I visit the pictures at the police station to see who is in trouble that I could help. Helping them, I help myself. Can you arrange for me to meet James? *Voila*, your brother is my brother."

"So, that's why you keep asking about him. I wondered. You better let me talk to him first. The pantyhose would throw him for a loop. He's a straight arrow since he returned to the straight and narrow." A ragtag musician serenaded them *sans* an invitation, upsetting the linen on her lap. Not having sufficient funds to tip him, she offered him a hit of wine. He took it.

"Torture is a perfectly lovely way to extract a confession on a vulgar Sunday afternoon. There is a ledge well suited for the job along the Gallery of the Gargoyles at Notre Dame."

Laughter disgorged from Seabright's stomach. "If I didn't like you so much, I'd swear you were the devil himself. Maybe the devil has a ponytail, not a pointy tail." She held her hands to the outdoor heat lamp to warm them, wishing the artists could enjoy such amenities.

Robespierre stuck his finger inside the lamp. "Behind the cross *is* the devil."

"I know Cervantes said that, but he also said, 'He who reads and travels much, sees and knows a great deal.'" She patted herself on the back playfully. "Since you didn't attribute Cervantes' quote to Cervantes, it seems I caught you stealing again, mister minister."

"As I did you."

She smiled to concede her guilt without acknowledging it.

"Cervantes also warned black sheep like you who go for wool often come home shorn."

"Like Matisse, I see black as a color. Eccentricity is its own inspiration, right?"

"I fear I have taught you well, *mademoiselle.* The surrealist Salvador Dali painted up here, and his *chef-d'oeuvre* was a graphic image of Christ looking down from the cross. His wooden death beam pushes back the veil of darkness that supposedly covered the earth."

"Supposedly? Jesus didn't come to earth for a vacation, unless you redefined vacation."

Tourists stampeded the square like The Running of the Bulls at Pamplona, threatening to purchase even the wet paintings after being trapped on a ten-countries-in-ten-days tour. Their bus finally broken down, affording them the opportunity to escape. "Montmartre derived its name, *mons martyrium*, from the martyrs who were tortured here in Paris," Robespierre explained.

"Your grasp of history is no match for my grasp of histrionics," she tittered.

"Beware, the devil is civil when flattered. Are you enjoying the devil's brew, my pretty?"

She blushed like a virgin on a honeymoon. "*Oui*, and I'm glad you think I'm pretty."

"Not everything you do is pretty. *Ca Ira,* it will be all right like they said in the French Revolution. One devil does not gouge out the eyes of another; the devil is good to his own."

"The devil takes his own too. Tell me more about Paris' history before James does."

"Place du Tertre was once the site of an abbey gallows, but martyrdom makes no sense to me. Why die? Why die to self, either? To me, the cross is a symbol of the power incarnate in all of us. God put Paris' last vineyard up here on Montmartre to reward artists for their rebellion."

"But many artists drink themselves to death, so why would God make Himself a party to partying?" she asked, confident he could come up with an answer that was a party in itself.

"It is a paradox like all Parables. All deep truths are marinated in madness."

Feeling frisky on account of the alcohol, the ambiance and an avant-garde priest, Seabright squeezed his thigh. "For a man with a frock, you're quite a shock, but Parker is wrong about you. You're not as mixed up as a tossed salad and every bit as fruity."

He threw his ponytail over his shoulder disgustedly. "That pig that Jesus cast the demons into is probably Parker's idea of a deviled ham, but I am a deviled ham, I am I am."

"Parker calls alcohol an *agent provocateur*, but you're an *agent provocateur* in the flesh. Everything you say is the opposite of what I was taught. I need more alcohol to appreciate it."

He clinked their glasses together. "*A votre sante!* The ancients called wine the blood of the gods, so we can better understand God when we drink the gods' blood *a la* communion."

"Drinking feels more like a blood covenant with the devil," she mumbled nervously.

"*Au contraire,* it only feels that way because your intellect is climbing to greater heights of spiritual understanding the way the

French funicular ascends to the summit of Montmartre. Like three-dimensional views to the eye of one who has looked only upon the printed page, it will take some time before your basilica of self-enlightenment feels *naturel*."

She tried to guess how many glasses of gods' blood they could get out of one carafe. No matter, it wouldn't be enough. It would never be enough. "Doesn't the Bible forbid fornication?"

"I do not concern myself much with the Bible. Why do you not call sex *sex*?"

"Why do you not call sin *sin*?" She hid her smirk behind the overpriced Montmartre menu. "Father, I think we choose to be oblivious to the obvious for obvious reasons."

"You have a healthy rebellion. Hide it not, for rebellion is the father of the future."

Wanting to play, she continued to spare. "Isn't 'healthy rebellion' an oxymoron?"

"No. Conformity is constipation. *Epater les bourgeois!*" He toasted the occasion, not caring that wine dribbled from his mustache. "Montmartre played host to many irreverent spirits whose nihilism birthed our Bohemian spirits. When we die, we shall have to thank them."

She fingerpainted purple swirls with the puddle of wine, but some property in the wine made her want to add her own blood to the mix. "Rebellion isn't like the sin of witchcraft?"

"Not if you are a good witch," Robespierre parried with a wink.

"A *good* witch? Now, that's incontestably an oxymoron." She stared at the oasis of easels, hoping to be able to rent a room that overlooked the artists' square. Uninvited concern nipped at her countenance, so she drank up as much as she could keep down so the fear wouldn't do any damage to her good time. "I've never seen a preacher scrap Scripture the way you do."

"Like I told you in the garden of dead bodies, God is bigger than the Bible, so if you want to understand God, close your Bible. *Comprenez-vous*? All real artists are anarchists."

She rocked back in her chair while drinking in the Montmartre moment, savoring the French wine on her table and the Bohemian music in the air. "I am learning so much from you."

"No, you are unlearning. You must write your own Scriptures, *mademoiselle.*"

"I'd kill to be a part of your flock, to live life without worrying about death, without worrying about hell. Life would be one big party for which God would pick up the tab!"

"My flock might get fleeced. When the devil preaches, the End is near," he teased.

The dimples disappeared from her apple blossom cheeks. "There must not be an End, and even if there is, it can't be near. That would spoil everything."

"Don't worry. When the End comes, my sheep shall not see it coming."

"That's more frightening! If the devil is coming for me, I want to know about it!"

"*Est-ce vrai?* What the devil delivers to your doorstep, he steals from your stoop."

"You don't think I'm a bad Christian, do you? If you can't debunk the Bible, my ass is grass." She gulped, not liking the taste of fear. "I said the sinner's prayer so I'm ok, right?"

"Wrong." He pulled his gypsy jewelry out of his flower-power vest and dangled it in front of her. "'The Spirit of the Lord has departed from you and become your enemy.'" He primped his blouse sleeves as if a model of good breeding. "That is what your Bible says."

Her chest felt as if it were imploding. "But not much in the Bible applies to *moi* today, *oui*? That's what I unlearned from you." Her eyes gravitated to the metal emblem that dangled from his neck like bait on a lure. "That's not like any cross I've ever seen. Is it French?"

"Translyvanian." A vendor wheeled a smelly cart of roasted chestnuts to their table.

Her eyes didn't leave the emblem. "Does the pentagram mean something different here?"

"*Oui, vive la difference!* It's the scholar's cross. A Renaissance scholar discovered that it is the symbol of Christ's execution that actually attracts demons. The devil's cross is what keeps the devil at a distance." He lifted the shiny metal circle off his neck and offered it to her.

Her button eyes came unbuttoned. "Maybe you *are* a wolf in sheep's clothing."

He leaned into her body. "Sheep don't wear any clothing." He tucked a rogue chestnut inside his floral turtleneck like an unsightly Adam's apple. "A wolf picks its prey from the sheep that have already been counted. It is *tres* easy to snatch a sheep that strays from the flock."

"Do all Europeans have such a dark sense of humor, *Pere* Robespierre?"

He slid toward her like a gator. "Darkness is just a different form of light."

"I can't follow the course of this conversation. Thank God you're recording it."

He made a pillow for her out of her book bag. "I joke about wolves and devils, but really I am a humble parish priest who wishes to save your brother from the guillotine of his guilt."

She sat up with a start. "Can we pa-leeaassseee not discuss James? I don't want to ruin this romantic rendezvous unless we can't think of anything better to do." Another street painter stopped at their outdoor table, offering to sketch their caricatures for a nominal fee. Apparently the number wasn't nominal enough for Robespierre, however. He lifted his boot to the man's sketch pad, threatening to topple it if he didn't exit, stage left. Seabright, on the other hand, empathized with the starving steward of creativity since she was also being consumed by starving desires. "Father, can you tell me more about your for-fornication theology?" she bleated.

Robespierre batted the baubles on his headband back and forth as if a tennis match were going on inside his head. "Sex is a gift from God, *sans souci.* No fruit is forbidden."

She used the wine to drown her doubt, but it also stoked her courage. "But if you think something isn't a sin, you won't repent of it before you die. Eternity is too long to be wrong."

"*Sacre bleu.*" His mood shifted like water under ice. "Are you a *homo unius libri?*"

Her face contorted itself with pained confusion. She swung her leg coquettishly, hoping to look more sophisticated than sophomoric. "There's not a perverted bone in my body."

"Nothing is perverted if you like it. God expects you to enjoy the desires She gave you."

"*Au contraire, Pere* Robespierre. Seven different passages in the Bible addressed to different cultures during different centuries condemn perversion. Try Jude 7 on for size."

"*Bouche cousue!*" He framed her face with his fingers. "You are well read on this subject. Why? Has someone close to you opened this gift? Your brother, perhaps?"

"No, I had to do a paper on the gay gospel at Civitas Dei. James is Mister Natural."

"*Au naturel*? Perhaps the victim spurned him, and that is his motive for murder."

"That's pretty far-fetched, even for you. He's a shotputter, so if someone was hit with a ball, he was probably showing off with it. What was that French phrase you called me?"

He knuckled her head. "It's Latin. *Homo unius libri* means 'man of one book.' It refers to monomaniacal morons who focus on the Bible to the exclusion of all other books."

"You'll be happy to know I haven't picked up my Bible once since I met you."

"That explains why you could thank God for something you stole."

Reviewing her visit to Paris in the movie chamber of her mind, she couldn't recall seeing him anywhere before the Brasserie Diable Agneau. "So, should I read the Bible or not?"

"Not. Reading the Bible's *ancien* letters is like reading other people's mail."

She crossed her feet at the ankles, letting the breeze tousle her hair as she daydreamed of being wildly happy. But she knew she wouldn't believe in the morning what she didn't dispute at night, so she refueled her glass as well as her skepticism. "Didn't Saint Paul say *all* Scripture is given by inspiration of God and is profitable for doctrine, reproof, correction and instruction?"

"Paul's views about sex are not Holy Writ," he scoffed with fiery condescension.

"But Scripture refers to his writings as Scripture. 2 Peter 3:15-16. Jesus validated the authority of Scripture every time He cited it, saying, 'It is written.' Not even Jonah is a fish tale."

He flicked the chestnut at her, smiling. "*Embarras du choix!* Love *is* love."

"But sex *is* sex, too. You're not pretending they're the same, are you?"

"Jesus started the sexual revolution. He let the woman caught in adultery go free."

"But He said 'Go and sin no more.' He didn't say adultery wasn't a sin."

Robespierre rotated his hand as if flipping flapjacks. "*Sic et Non,* yes and no. That book by the Parisian Peter Abelard exposed many errors in the Church. He was castrated for breaking his vow of celibacy. That is why I do not share my enlightenment with just anyone. I could lose my *elan vital.* It was the backwards Church that linked sexuality to reproduction."

She wanted to drink, not think. "But doesn't one naturally lead to the other?"

"The definition of natural will change. Truth was not written in stone."

"There were those two stone tablets that Moses picked up on Mount Sinai..."

He drew a heart on her souvenir menu. "Love is the only Law. Do what thou will."

"'Do what thou will' is from the satanic bible. It mocks our 'Thou shalt not' list. Either way, your logic is so subjective it's subject to abuse. If I wanted your mate, I could ditch mine to hitch thine." Staring into his cool, black eyes, she felt like ditching everything for him.

"*Si jeunesse savait, femme fatale. Cherie,* in 1616 the Church declared heliocentricism to be contrary to the Bible and made Galileo recant, so not all truth lines up with the Bible."

"The Church was wrong, not the Bible. If the Bible is wrong, it's right to do wrong, right?" Feeling giddy about the prospects his new interpretations presented, she didn't want to argue too hard lest she win. Her head kept swirling, but she hoped to give it another swirlie.

"Christ died to make us free, did He not? Cervantes taught us that."

"That's a Bible verse, stupid."

"Don't call me stupid. Call me evil if you wish, but not stupid." He patted the dew on his pumpkin head as if he were accustomed to requiring honesty from his parishioners, not himself.

Her fresh face soured as she swallowed a yawn, hoping it didn't betray her inexperience.

"You're not a day drinker, I see. Can I interest you in a nipper's nap inside Sacre Coeur?"

"That sounds like a plan, but I'm so sleepy, it could be dark when I wake up."

"It could be dark *where* you wake up." He stabbed her with his plastic pitchfork. "Do know I'm only kidding, love. This priest does not even believe in hell."

"I'm going to have to drink a lot more than this to appreciate your level of apostasy. You are a pastor who drinks, undermines the Bible, favors fornication, and doesn't believe in hell? Or do you not believe in hell because you drink, undermine the Bible and favor fornication?"

He raised his knife. "You are on to me, now I shall have to kill you. *Sauve-qui-peut!*"

She dropped a chestnut down his shirt. "You said that before. What does it mean?"

"You will remember when you wake up, *if* you wake up," he teased.

CHAPTER EIGHT

Sacre Coeur, Montmartre
8:20 p.m. 22 February

Seabright felt her way along the cold marble floor. "Where am I?"

"In a crypt, of course," Robespierre replied.

She scoured her eyes, disoriented by the darkness and the fantastical shapes that moved in and out of focus like tiles in a kaleidoscope. "Why aren't these people moving? Is that a body?"

He blew out the candle behind her. "Did those statues have you fooled for a moment?"

A bizarre form moved toward her like animated smoke. "What happened?"

"Before or after you rode around and around the neon windmill at the Moulin Rouge?"

She felt something sticky under her elbow like blood. "Tell me I didn't."

"You did." He relit the candle and held it under his face like a jaundiced jack-o-lantern.

"Why can't I remember?"

He made a drinking motion. "You also confessed to your brother's murder."

"You mean the murder my brother committed, right?"

"Wrong. You confessed that you murdered your brother. I have it on tape."

"But my brother isn't dead."

"Not yet…"

She felt herself wobbling. "God told me to leave it behind, or I'd be left behind."

"Leave what behind?"

She made a drinking motion of her own, her head banging like a church bell. "The killer could've been watching me all along, and I wasn't even watching out for him."

He made binoculars of his fingers. "Funny you should mention that. A guy wearing wingtips and a wool coat wrapped you in his coat when you passed out in Place du Tertre."

She gasped in horror. "You let a weirdo in wingtips and a wool coat wrap me up after I told you the creep at the Eiffel Tower was wearing wingtips and a wool coat?"

"This weirdo had teeth like a train wreck, one leg and one eye. I doubt it's the same guy."

"Not funny. Parker warned this would happen. I started listening to your liberal crap, so I was out like a light when the killer came calling! How is it I'm even alive right now?"

"Maybe he needs you to be alive to testify against your dead brother."

Her body shook uncontrollably. "Stop it. Why didn't you just take me home?"

"I didn't know where home was. I still don't."

"You know my uncle's apartment overlooks Montmartre Cemetery."

"As do thousands of apartments. *Mon Dieu*, I would have been arrested had I tried to drag your body through Montmartre Cemetery in the dark. I know, I tried it with another girl."

"You are so very droll, but I guess droll is better than dishonest, and politeness is just a rehearsed sort of dishonesty." Muffled voices echoed across the area above her, but the air remained damp and silent all around her.

"I know that weirdo with the wingtips you saw at the Eiffel. His name is Hawk Devlin."

"Why didn't you say so sooner? 'Hawk' is an alias if ever I've heard one."

"Hawk is a drifter and a grifter. I should have suspected you'd hook up with him eventually, given your propensity to take what does not belong to you, *mademoiselle*."

Seabright grabbed his arm. "Are you being nasty or is it just my imagination?"

"Nasty."

She laughed despite her fear. "How do you know this Hawk grifter-drifter guy?"

"I met him on a wine country tour. Hawk cruises the tours looking for suckers with more dollars than sense. If you see him again, I rather think you should steer clear of him."

"Thank you for the fatherly advice, father. Hawk didn't lay a hand on me?"

"A coat but not a hand. You must not be the man he wants."

"Why are you acting as if this was no big deal? He could have killed me!"

"You do not know that he killed anyone, and I did not know he was the man you loaned your pen to since you are much in the habit of 'borrowing.' Do you know how many weirdos in Paris wear a wool coat and wingtips? They all do. This man didn't do anything suspicious. Was I supposed to arrest him for wearing a three-piece suit to a two-bit bistro?"

The bells started ringing in Sacre Coeur's belltower which looked like a fat rocket too content with itself to blast off. "Did I hear nine bells? No wonder it's dark out."

"The sound of church bells tormented Faust once he sold his soul to the devil…"

"The church bells must torment you, too, but they sure don't torment Parker. He's the only person I know for sure is going up when lowered into the ground."

Robespierre ran his finger down the middle of her back just to see if she would flinch. "I believe whatever mythic realm awaits our *immortalite,* we shall all get there *finalement.* At least we are not milling about the landscape where the killer struck last time."

"*Last* time? Do you think he's a serial killer? That's way scarier!"

"That's what a gargoyle whispered in my ear during an out-of-body voyage."

"Stop with the jokes." The glowing shapes looked like sci-fi creatures in the darkness. "It's dark, I'm hungover, and I'm going to Parker's place that is so dry it's a fire hazard."

"Parker sounds like Tolstoy's Pierre in *War and Peace*. He only feels strong when he's absolutely pure. *S'il vous plait*, are you now going to acquaint yourself with abstinence?"

"Why? You're a pastor and you drink, so I figure if you can get through the Pearly Gates with Perignon in hand, I can too. Mind you, I only drink when I'm afraid...afraid I'm not going to have any fun! What's this crap about my brother? What do you know that I don't know?"

"Rather a lot, I'm afraid. My ingenious ingenue popped him off, did she not?"

"No way, *Pere* Parfait. And I'm in no mood for your sick jokes."

"Your Bible says hate is like murder in the heart, so you murdered him."

"I'll light a pray-for-the-person candle if that sin bothers you so much when all the other ones don't, but my mouth is as dry as an Egyptian tomb, so I'm out of here, *pere*."

"I dare say, it's that colossal mosaic of Christ that is still bothering you, isn't it."

"Maybe. It makes me afraid to just go out and do whatever I want to do."

"Indubitably, my ingenue."

"Quit calling me that!" She swung her bag at him but missed.

"My, we are dreadfully cranky when reality returns, are we not? I rather gather it was altogether too higgledy-piggledy for you in Pigalle tonight. At least you stopped crying, love."

Seabright wished the darkness included a movie screen that would play back the parts of the evening she couldn't remember since she'd obviously done things she wanted to forget. *It must have been fun while it lasted. No one can take my Montmartre memories away from me, even if I can't remember what they are right now...*

"Are you quite all right?" he asked, deliberately dripping candle wax on her wrist.

"That stupid temptation termination card is probably prophetic," she grumbled, her heart pounding. "It's *tres* true, wine does take away the heart and spiritual understanding."

"*Au contraire. In vino veritas*, remember?"

"No, I don't remember. That's the problem, one in a series of escalating problems. Give me that light and I'll show you one of the pathetic, prophetic Scripture cards Parker made for me so that I'd fly instead of fry." She rubbed her eyes as he passed her the tiny torch. Reaching inside her book bag, her fingers happened on a strange leaflet. "This is a rather cowardly way to give me a spiritual spanking," she carped, her head thumping like a broken water pump.

"A nun dropped that in there, I didn't. You were sound asleep, so I left it alone."

"I can't believe you let me sleep so long that it's dark out." She unfolded the colorful brochure designed to look like a Sacre Coeur mosaic. "No nun would go through my things."

"She didn't go through them. She thought she was doing you a favor."

"You clerics always cover for each other. The prayer on the back is printed in English, so I can't just blow it off or God might blow me off. *Sacre bleu!* This is the very same verse that Parker put on a temptation termination card. Cold coincidence! 'If you do not do well, sin is crouching at the door.' I was already hungover, now I have to feel guilty on top of it?"

"Not if you listen to me. Ministers should not use fear to control people."

"I don't fear anything when I'm drinking, not even God," she laughed even though she was about to heave all the hooch she had. "You don't think I need to quit?"

"Of course not. God is the giver of life, and drinking makes you feel alive, does it not?"

"Not right now. I feel like death. Maybe nunny is just trying to keep my fanny out of the fire, same as Parker. Left to my own devices, I'd probably be in the pitchfork pyre already."

He held the leaflet to the flame. "What if there is no fire? No sin? No devil?"

"Then there is no God, and only God knew I'd be up here doing this tonight."

"Doing what? We are recreating, not procreating. *Laissez-les jouer ensemble.*"

The candlelight began to fade again. "Hearing these same verses from two sources can't be a coincidence. It's God, all right. I don't remember some stuff, so I wasn't in control."

"*C'est impossible* to be in control *toujours* of your dreams? Dreams are their own Scripture," he instructed her while burning the Scripture leaflet before her eyes.

She arched her back until it cracked. "You are good at finding exceptions to every rule."

"That is why you chose me. Doubt is not the enemy of faith, it *is* faith. Tolstoy said, 'Doubts on which he tried not to dwell stirred in his soul.' Doubt is a *funiculare* to faith."

"I doubt doubt is the virtue you make it out to be."

His nostrils flared like a gorilla's. "You gather your wits about you frightfully fast."

"Mortal terror will do that to you." Seabright wished she could see the bright blue sky and happy ice cream domes of Sacre Coeur instead of a dizzying darkness. "I bet if I thought something was black my whole life, you could convince me it's white."

"*Tres bien.* It is a gift. I shall pass it on to you."

She checked her bag for other nasty surprises. "The Bible warns about pastors who call darkness light, and light darkness. That Scripture is also on my temptation termination card."

She tried to show him the Scripture, but he refused it like a dirty tissue. "Fear is very unevolved, *mademoiselle*. It is the *sine qua non* of all pagan religions."

"No offense, but you are pagan, aren't you?" she goaded him.

A ghoulish grin spread across his face. "If love is pagan, I am pagan. *C'est impossible* to dive into the depths of love while foundering in the shallows of fear."

"*Tres* true, you can't enjoy love and fear at the same time. They are distinct pleasures. I just know I'm not afraid with you, so I'm afraid I've become involuntarily enamored with you."

"And I, you." His words echoed across the cold crypt walls. "You put too much faith in the Bible and too little in yourself. Smell the pungent incense and votive candles, hear the sonorous chants—this is the spirituality you need, a spirituality without any printed words."

She sniffed and sniffed. "All I can smell is the wine I spilled on my pants."

"Your wounded heart spilled out of your eyes, that is all." His face looked cold and hard like the marble in the mortuary. "One heart has already been buried in Sacre Coeur's crypt."

"Is that why they sell tickets to descend into Sacre Coeur's Stygian darkness?"

"A country that charges you to use the toilet sees nothing wrong with selling tickets to lesser pleasures." Robespierre leaned backwards, but both of his knees popped in protest.

"You are unforgettably fun, and fun is my *raison d'etre* right now, but I've sampled enough naughtiness for one night, and I need to get home before Parker calls the cops."

"Just click your heels three times and say, 'There's no place like home.'"

"There's no place like Paris, that's for sure. I'm having myself a real adventure."

"Adventures are their own *rites de passage*." He led her through the crypt's shadowy columns and arches with his arm around her shoulder. She wanted his arm to be around her waist, because the shoulder thing felt too fatherly for someone whom she hoped would father her children. "*Apres vous*. I know a shortcut to the cemetery, but it's underground."

"I don't know Paris well enough to go underground at night."

"I do. Trust me." He escorted her outside where equestrian statues stood on top of Sacre Couer's wedding cake facade like giant hood ornaments. The moon hovered dangerously close to the church's Byzantine belltower like a balloon that wanted to impale itself on the illuminated turret. "In case you have a go at swooning again, I best know your address, love. Maybe your brother and I can have that chat tonight. I'll take him to the tombs and torture a confession out of him," Robespierre laughed while skipping merrily down the steps.

She froze two steps short of him. "I told you, it's best if I speak with him first."

"There is no time like the present...."

She ratcheted her head around, thinking he looked rather bass-mouthed and homely under the lights, and did his arms not look like a gibbon's? "Tame James is not even at Parker's place right now. He went to some historical site today, probably Versailles or Verdun."

"Then I invite both of you to join me on a *bateau mouche* tomorrow night."

Robespierre looked like a walrus advanced in age more than intellect, but she knew there would be good chemistry between them again as soon as there were good chemicals between them again. "If you insist upon James coming, why not invite my uncle and ruin everything?"

"Another time, *s'il vous plait.* It is possible only to extract confessions *tete-a-tete.*"

CHAPTER NINE

Chez Chateau, The Right Bank
5:20 p.m. 23 February

"The dining room has a drawbridge, the kitchen is surrounded by a moat, and the can looks like a castle? Why did you pick a palace like this to party in?" Seabright complained with a sophomoric snottiness that was festering into full blown French snobbishness.

"Funky fiddlesticks, I thought you'd like it," James stammered, as intimidated by her as by their mother who was a swollen version of her. "Don't these make-believe battlements take you back in time to Old World France? It feels like a war could break out any minute."

"History is as dead as Parker's neighbors." She studied the local fashions to know which knock-offs to buy. "Speaking of the dead, did you hear about the death at the Eiffel Tower?"

He didn't look as surprised as she expected. "Don't keep me in suspense."

She pushed her gum around her mouth, realizing any confession was a crapshoot since his loyalty had always been only to himself. "I was in the neighborhood the night of the murder."

"So was I."

"So I heard."

"You did?"

"*Oui.*" She drummed the tabletop with her fingers. "Why don't you tell me what happened before my priest-pal shows up so you can beat feet after your meet-and-greet?"

"It's nice to know I'm not a wanted man in your book, but it's not safe to talk here, sis. Somebody might overhear us. That's why I've been trying to catch up with you at Parker's."

"Parker is the one person I don't want to overhear my conversations. His narrow world view could wreck this broad's big dreams," she laughed, intoxicated by her reckless courage. "This eating establishment is so stiff I bet the food is prepared on embalming tables."

"After what happened at the Eiffel Tower, I'm done embalming myself. I've been training my whole life but choosing to party in Paris could cost me my Olympic eligibility. Satan's game plan for my life is death, and I'm not punting my future into his paws."

"Not everyone is an athlete, brother dearest."

"You're a Christian, so you're supposed to be a spiritual athlete."

"I don't know that I'd call myself a Christian any more."

"Let me guess, your priest-pal doesn't call himself a Christian any more either, right?"

She glared at him as if had just read her locked diary. "Robespierre led me into a cocoon of enlightenment, and I won't let you clip my wings before I get clearance for takeoff. Taking every thought into captivity felt like captivity. I feel free for the first time in my life."

"Deception will do that to you. Deception *is* drunkenness, you know."

"France is fun, so I'll take my chances. Thoreau said we live but a fraction of our lives."

"We live but a fraction of our lives *on earth.* We'll enjoy, or endure, eternity elsewhere."

She blew a bubble then popped it with her tongue to get him to back off. "My hero, Hemingway, said, 'I can't stand to think my life is going by so fast and I'm not really living it.'"

"Your hero was so worried about not living his life that he ended it."

"Very funny. The point is, I feel totally alive with this priest, dangerously alive."

"You feel so alive that you didn't notice another man's death?"

"I couldn't help but notice it, but I had nothing to do with it. Did you?"

"Of course not."

"Then why were you acting so strange the night of the murder?"

"Why are you acting so strange now?"

"I guess it is strange for a Christian to be happy, isn't it. Nietzsche was right when he said 'The Christian faith from the beginning is sacrifice, the sacrifice of all freedom, all pride, all self-confidence of spirit; it is at the same time subjection, a self-derision, and self-mutilation.'"

"Since when did Nietzsche become your hero, sis?"

"Nietzsche is Robespierre's hero, Robespierre is my hero, and I've never been happier. You can't argue with that." She studied her Seine map. "He's introduced me to many French writers. Voltaire wrote: 'Doubt isn't a pleasant mental state, but certainty is a ridiculous one.'"

"Doubt is ridiculous for a pastor to defend. Uncertainty isn't as sophisticated as it sounds, sis. One fudges the truth when one is full of fudge. Pastors are human; Scripture is divine."

She bent her fingers backward until they cracked. "Must you be so negative?"

"Truth isn't negative or positive, it only seems negative when you are positive you don't want to hear it." James hid his hands in his chinos which he wore to impress her.

She ground her teeth like sandpaper. "This is turning into a Brobdingnagian bummer."

"Sorry. What do you like best about Paris? The alligator-shaped *baguettes*?"

"Not this sirloin shrine to chauvinism, that's for sure. I like the wine cellars that put their bottles up for adoption behind protective glass windows like babies in a maternity ward."

"I noticed the chic shops wear wraparound wrought-iron balconies while the rattier dives have fake balconies that look like kennels whose pets were liberated long before Paris ever was."

"It figures you'd home in on Paris' architecture instead of its Enlightenment."

"The architecture talks to me the way the literature talks to you, sis."

"Robespierre says, 'Art is all that cannot be suppressed.'"

"Modern art is all that should be," James muffled his laughter with the menu.

"Not funny. The Fauvists designed visual adrenalin with their irreverent colors. Rebellion was their *raison d'etre.* Cubism, surrealism, and expressionism were the eye-popping result."

"A Dadaist thought he could convert a urinal into a work of art by signing it. Another modernist titled a red square *Red Square.* This jock only goes to bat for French Impressionism."

"I didn't know you knew anything about French Impressionism."

"Everyone knows something about French Impressionism whether they know it or not."

"Art hurts, but it hurts real good." She recoiled, disgusted that she was disclosing any part of her heart to him. "Why am I talking to you? You think jockstraps are *joie de vivre.*"

"I never met a water lily I liked, but I love sunshine filtered through big aqua waves and Monet's color in motion. French Impressionism feels real good when I feel real bad."

"This does not compute on the monitor of my mind. Tomorrow I'm doing the Louvre."

"Parker loves the Louvre. You could find out from him what's worth seeing."

"I have no intention of finding out anything from him. Be glad he's not here so we can do some things we'll regret," she snickered like fire racing for gasoline. "'Fun' isn't in his lexicon."

"He's a biker, so just getting to work is fun for him. The best fun to be had at the Louvre in my jock strap opinion is decoding the little paintings painted inside the big paintings."

"Don't tell me anything else about the Louvre. You're ruining it for me."

A waiter marched by with the remains of a chicken, its head having succumbed to the same fate as Marie Antoinette. "I went to Versailles yesterday, but our guide should've passed out clothespins on the coach. The rooms stuck so bad you'd swear old furniture can fart."

She peered down her nose contemptuously at him, though this was no easy feat since her nose had taken an upturn upon arriving in Paris. "You have such *savoir faire,* brother drearest."

"I'm a veritable culture vulture. Did you know Napolean owned 44 palaces? He tried to build the first tunnel under the English Channel, too. Isn't that interesting?"

"Not at all." She retouched her lipstick as if kissing were the only thing on her mind.

James escorted her around the restaurant with his eyes. "I hoped you'd be smitten with the murals of medieval Paris, the exquisite guild windows, the richly illuminated prayer books, the tapestry wallpaper, the manor house tables, and the waitresses with the two-foot-tall hats." His eyes visited a display of swords as he contemplated what a sawlike claymore could do to Hawk if he ran into him again on a dark night in a dark neighborhood in a dark mood.

"Europeans are so cosmopolitan. My *bon vivant* speaks French half the time, British English half the time, and Hollywood slang half the time."

"Your math is suspect, sis."

"Not as suspect as you are," she sniped, knowing a finger of accusation would be pointed at her if she didn't give him the finger first. "A witness picked your face out of a crowd."

James blinked incredulously. "What does this witness look like?"

"An artist on holiday. He wears pantyhose, Pantaloons and a ponytail."

"He sounds like a she."

"No, he's a man, a man of God, but he's big into slumming and bumming like a Bohemian Bolshevik. He wears a big broom mustache and baubled headband, too."

"The Eiffel Tower killer is just the opposite, conservative and clean-shaven."

"Was he wearing a wool coat and wingtips?"

James scratched his chin with the medieval menu. "Could be. I'm no fashion diva."

Seabright leaned toward him. "Would his name happen to be Hawk Devlin?"

"How on earth did a late arrival to Paris like you know a name like that?"

"Father Robespierre knows him."

"That figures. Hawk is probably one of his disciples, the disciple whom he loves."

She tossed her menu at him with self-righteous disgust. "Are you sure the dead guy was a victim of foul play?" she asked to erase any lingering doubt about her culpability.

"Yes. He got whacked by a bowling ball, a lawn bowling ball of all things."

"You actually saw Hawk Devlin kill him?" she gasped.

"No." He held the menu sideways. "Shhhh! Somebody might understand English."

"Then how do you know he did it?"

"He bragged to me that he did it."

She pushed the menu into his chest. "Did you report this to the police?"

"I made a statement anonymously to the authorities, but Hawk is capable of framing both of us for the murder, so I didn't want to risk getting either of us arrested for something we didn't do. I know he's out there somewhere. He's probably watching us as we speak."

"He can't frame me. I don't even know him."

"Hawk said Little Red Riding Hood gave him a Civitas Dei College pen and Civitas Dei paper, and he jammed her pen into the victim's thigh before writing a fake suicide note on Little Red's paper. I feared it was you on the tower that night."

She looked as dazed as a rollercoaster rider. "Why didn't you warn me, James?"

"I did, but you denied being there. I figured one of us lost a pen. Besides, other women wear capes. I told you someone was murdered at the Eiffel, and I begged you not to go out alone. The cops are going to assume you're hiding something since you didn't come forward."

"You didn't make a full confession, either. You phoned in your tip anonymously."

"The cops know how to reach me through an intermediary," James explained. "Since I saw the killer up close and personal, I didn't want to leave a forwarding address. I'm already a target. There's no sense in making myself an *easy* target, Danielle."

"Don't call me Danielle. You know I'm calling myself Seabright now." Her countenance softened when she realized she could lose her brother. As much as she hated him, she loved him, too. "Is that why you're deliberately sprouting those chin hairs? Is that shaveable camouflage?"

"Exactly." He felt his stubble, knowing it was entirely inadequate but hoping she wouldn't be so unkind as to tell him so. "I also bought this artsy-fartsy beret on the Left Bank."

"It's not you."

"That's why I bought it. This peacoat belongs to Parker. My Civitas Dei jacket could've been a dead giveaway, literally. Parker's leather *lederhosen* were too tight for my tush."

Seabright grilled him like a burger. "Did you tell Parker what you saw?"

"Yeah, yesterday."

She flipped the burger over. "What is he doing about it?"

"Praying, you know Parker. I made him my lawyer before blabbing to him to keep him from going to the cops, but the lawyer in him says I should pay the cops a personal visit."

"Pay 'em a visit then back-paddle across the Big Pond until the coast is clear."

"Maybe I should, but probably I won't, not until World Competition is over. Like I told you, track and field pays big bucks in Europe. If I don't make the Olympics, I need to cash in some chips over here before settling for selling insurance back home."

"Having a free place to stay doesn't hurt."

"Guilty as charged, as are you."

"I'm not doing guilt these days." Her eyes focused on the inlaid mosaic tabletop because it was infinitely easier to look at than the face of someone who was challenging her choices. "If the killer is looking for you, doesn't that throw a monkey wrench into your shot-put pit?"

"More like a blown engine. This Hawk guy is sharp as a nail gun, and his eyes are every bit as piercing. If I ever look into those eyes again, I bet they'll be the last thing I see."

Seabright wanted to hide behind her hair, but she didn't want to miss Robespierre if he swaggered by one of the archers' windows. "What on earth happened that night?"

James glanced over his shoulder while noting the saber nearest him. "You know I don't drink, but this guy in our French class talked two of us into doing this chateaux and champagne tour. Next thing you know, one guy is dead and the other guy killed him."

"Verbal volleyball isn't usually a full contact sport. What went wrong?"

"We were drinking, so the possibilities are infinite, sis," he confessed with a penitential peace. "All I know is he set me up to take the fall for a murder, and he set you up, too."

"Hawk Devlin sounds like an alias intended to intimidate. Devlin sounds like devil, unless he's using it like a verb, as in devilin'. Hawk is obviously an allusion to his predatory nature."

"Danielle Seabright, your keen intellect is no match for your rabid imagination."

"Look up Hawk Devlin in the phone book. I bet you find jack squat. His alias tells us he's a gamester, so I wouldn't be surprised to learn he's playing cat-and-mouse with the cops."

"Hawk doesn't know I'm using my middle name as my last name. He thinks my name is James Woodlawn, not James Woodlawn Seabright. That might be saving my life right now."

Seabright wondered if Hawk knew she had transposed her first and last names. Staring into the rock-hewn fireplace, she realized she was also skating on thin ice. However, she was certain Robespierre could allay her fears after redefining skating, ice, and the prospects which falling through that ice presented. "How did this devil named Devlin do the dirty deed?"

"Hawk bonked him with a bowling ball the size of a shot-put."

"Somebody must have seen him do it. A million people mill around the Eiffel."

"That's what I thought as I went over the details in my mind." James rubbed his eyes as if trying to erase the image of a life being rubbed out. "There's even a cop shop under the Eiffel."

Seabright's cheeks puffed out like a blow fish as shock rocked her world. "What's the statute of limitations on petty theft?" she asked as if they were suddenly on the same team.

"This wasn't petty, and it wasn't a theft, sis."

She tried to cover her tracks. "Hawk stole a man's life, did he not?"

"Hawk took photos of me with the victim, he got my fingerprints on the evidence, and he made sure the cops saw me putting the dead guy's beret on a bench with the fake suicide note."

"Why were you so cuckoo-cooperative, James Woodlawn Seabright?"

"I half thought he might kill me, or you, if I didn't do as he said. I was in a daze from partying, so I wasn't thinking straight. Parker is right, everything catches up with everybody."

"Whatever." She glared at the inn's battlements, longing to see murals of the French Revolution, not medieval Paris. Medieval Paris was too religious for her new concept of God.

"Why would Hawk kill someone he just met at a stupid French class?"

"The night didn't start out with murder. First, he talked us into popping into some very velvety bars up in piggy Pigalle. As you know, the sewers of Paris are famous, but in Pigalle they're above ground. We thought the jaunt was a joke, but maybe it wasn't a joke to him."

"Since when is bar hopping gone bad a motive for murder?"

"Bar hopping begets its own motives. Hawk also threatened me that night."

"So, venturing off to Versailles yesterday must have been quite a risk for Tame James."

"*Oui,* but Parker helped me conceal my identity." He made a mask of his fingers. "Paris has been one big wake up call that made me take a second look at the Good Book."

"What's so good about it? I believe Cervantes is every bit as inspired as Scripture."

"Cervantes didn't seem to think so." Concern darkened his countenance. "I brought you another temptation termination card. I'd feel better knowing you had it with you."

"I'll take it, but only so I can show it to Robespierre," she groaned.

"I can get one for him."

"No, he'll get enough of a laugh out of this one."

James recoiled like a Napoleonic cannon. "Only sinister ministers laugh at Scripture."

Seabright cracked the lamination on the card, demonstrating her contempt for it.

"Sis, you used to quote the Bible to me when I was on a slippery slope of self-deception. Why do you hate the Bible now that I'm quoting it back to you?"

She tossed the card on the table then retouched her come-hither lipstick, hoping it would end up on the mouth of the man James loathed. "I really don't want to get into this with you."

He read from the card, ignoring her contempt. "Sin twice and it won't feel like sin."

She used her knife to spin the card around, determined to keep it at a safe distance, so it wouldn't ruin her unsafe intentions. "Stop sinning or something worse may happen to you."

"That's John 5:14 but you skipped Luke 21:34. 'Be on guard so your hearts aren't depressed with the giddiness and nausea of self-indulgence, drunkenness, and worldly worries…so that Day comes upon you suddenly like a trap.' Did you bring a Bible to Europe with you?"

She glared at the dark decor, ticked that she had to talk to a *homo unius libri*. "What's it to you? I'm thinking outside the box. Robespierre helped me see the *tabula rasa* I was at birth."

"I think you want to break the Tablets more than you want to be a blank one." The rhetoric in the room heated up as if flaming catapults had landed in the French fortress.

"Thanks for the oversimplification. I didn't get enough of that at Civitas Dei. Nietzsche taught us this: 'One's belief in truth begins with doubt of all truths one has believed hitherto.'"

"Nietzsche was no friend of God and no Christian."

"Does one have to be a Christian to be a friend of God?" she hooted.

"When your enemies become your friends, and your friends become your enemies, you're doing the *danse macabre*. You're deceived, sis."

Ticked that James knew some French phrases that she didn't know, she ground her teeth like java beans. "Nothing is forbidden. Ergo, the possibilities for my happiness are infinite."

"God is concerned about our holiness, not our happiness, although one often follows the other. You might be happy for a season, but damned for all eternity. Deception sets you up to take you down. How do you feel about that?"

"I couldn't be happier!"

James felt as if he were engaged in a battle that required spiritual weapons, not the medieval ones that surrounded them. "Even the gargoyles of Paris served a purpose, to channel rain off the roofs, but just because something serves a purpose in your life doesn't mean it wasn't Satan-sent. Some gorgeous people and places are mere conduits for evil."

She grasped her knife like a sword. "He happens to be part of a persecuted minority."

"The sexually immoral are not in the minority, not here and certainly not in hell. Here's one last Scripture, sis: 'Your sins have withheld good things from you.' Jeremiah 5:25."

"You sound like party pooper Parker. I think I'll move in with Robespierre." Her words were raised swords. "Tell the waiter this woman ain't gonna dine if she can't get no wine."

"I guess I should have asked you to meet me at one of Paris' spectacular churches."

"The whole world is now my church. I'm not parochial like Parker. I can find God wherever I will, like Loyola. Hurry up. Robespierre might be waiting on the quai already."

"Why does this rebellious revisionist want to meet me? I don't get it."

"He's a man of the cloth, and you're a man on the run."

"I'm not running from God, I'm running from the devil, or quite possibly the devil incarnate." He pantomime preached by racing his fingers across the medieval menu.

"Robespierre has keen insights about the devil and deception," she defended him.

"Why? Was he deceived once upon a time?"

"He still is," she laughed, her toes curling nervously inside her shoes.

"Then why are you befriending him?" James stood to leave. "Deception will take you to places you don't want to go and keep you longer than you want to stay. It's a holiday in hell."

"That's what you think." She whipped her cape over her shoulder like a matador.

Pink clouds huddled on the horizon like cotton candy. "Has Parker met this guy?"

"No." She fondled the ashtray, wanting to throw it at him. She didn't expect her baby brother to damage her clever theological constructs. "Robespierre wanted it to be just us three."

"Then it's a good thing I have the strength of two." James stretched out as if he had just stepped out of the suit of armor that stood at attention in the lobby. "I'm not letting you out of my sight after what you told me about this monster minister."

"Just because he doesn't think like you do doesn't mean he's a wolf in sheep's clothing."

"I hope not, sis, because Little Red Riding Hood didn't fair so well with the Big, Bad Wolf. Regardless, the Church should not be a playground for his rebellion. Satan will have the last laugh if he gets you to score a touchdown for the wrong team."

CHAPTER TEN

Aboard a bateau mouche, The Seine
7:12 p.m. 23 February

Seabright and 1,200 of her closest friends shuffled across the deck of a colossal *bateau mouche* sightseeing boat in search of the best views of Paris. For as far as the eye could see, floodlit fountains, Medieval turrets, Gothic facades, Baroque domes, Classical columns and Renaissance towers dressed the French shoreline along with one lonely Egyptian obelisk which cars circled frenetically like wasps around a hive. Cruising under the Belle Epoque's elegant Pont Alexandre III bridge with its Old World lanterns and sumptuous gold statuary, Seabright felt hellbent on enjoying all the night could offer.

When the popular Place de la Concorde popped into view, Robespierre made his way to the boat bar, prompting James to have a long-awaited word with his sister. "Seabright, if your priest-pal wants to talk to me so bad, why is he treating me like a *persona non grata*?"

Angry that a mere jock had a scholar's tongue, she replied, "He came to hear *you* talk."

"I tried, but apparently he's a man of few words."

She wished James would jump overboard. "I hope you didn't preach at him."

"I asked him a couple of questions about his spirituality, then he fluttered his hand and stared at me as if I were the ghost of the person who died at the Eiffel Tower."

"I bet Hawk wishes you were dead, but Robespierre is here to help you."

"I'm gambling on God's help, and gambling is hard work," he joked. Reaching for the bill of his ball cap, he found a beret instead.

"Sis, did you know the victim was wearing a beret? I took it off his dead head and set it on a bench with a bogus suicide note."

She looked at him as if he'd lost his marbles, though not the big marble she lost while sneaking up the Eiffel. "Why on earth did you do a dumb thing like that?"

"Because Hawk threatened to frame me for the murder if I didn't. Come to find out, he framed me for the murder because I *did.* Ice cubes are cuddly compared to him."

"Ice will melt in hell," she replied without taking her eyes off the scenery. "Where's my priest? I want his sterling commentary to ignite my river reveries before this ride is history."

"Maybe I can be of help," James offered. "If you'll look beyond the melodramatic statues on Bridge Alexandre, you'll see the Baroque dome under which Napolean was buried. That's Napolean's military academy to the right of his stately Hotel des Invalides, and that carpet of green which stretches from the Champ de Mars to the Eiffel Tower is Napolean's field of war."

"War, war, and more war. Is that the only language my brother understands?"

"No, but battle art intrigues me because it's a freeze frame of a country's feelings at pivotal moments in history, sis. Why do you assume athletes don't appreciate art?"

She flung her hair starboard. "You never spent a vulgar Sunday afternoon in a museum."

"I like the stuff on the outside, not the inside. Architecture is outside art. By the way, your French friend sounds as if he has the plague, so I kept my distance without backing into anyone on board wearing a wool coat and wingtips, if you know what I mean."

"I don't think Robespierre is going to give me his undivided attention until he's granted you his absolution, so get it over with, would you?" Seabright grumbled.

"I don't need his absolution. I already repented," James replied matter-of-factly.

"When? You were partying your ass off in Paris same as me until this happened."

He thought about her future instead of his past. "I was only a confession away from walking the walk again. You're only a confession away yourself. He doesn't seem to realize I'm your brother. You should have introduced us before jogging off to the john. To get the conversation rolling, I asked him where Princess Di crashed. He nodded perfunctorily at a Right Bank tunnel. I didn't know you could board a *bateau mouche* at Pont de l'Alma, so he asked me where I boarded one before. End of conversation."

"You didn't tell me you already went on a Seine cruise."

"That's how I eluded Hawk's steely grasp the night of the murder." James studied a woman in a wool coat and wingtips who was a good foot taller than Hawk and not nearly as clean-shaven. "I prayed for a way of escape using I Corinthians 10:13 that Parker printed on the back of each temptation termination card. A cruise boat was my trap door out of temptation."

"What temptation?" she scoffed, venom spitting across her vocal cords.

"I was tempted to shoot Hawk in the hind end with a *boules* ball when I realized he was framing me for murder. Granted, I wasn't exactly thinking clearly on account of the alcohol in my system, but such quaint conflict resolution did cross my mind."

She stared at the lights crisscrossing the liquid stage of the Seine. Illuminated buildings on the horizon promised an architectural feast in the near future. "Robespierre should've recognized you from that picture I showed him from Christmas at Cape Hatteras."

"I didn't look like this in that picture." James scratched his stubble as if it were a rash. "Then again, how well can anyone see through Coke-bottom glasses?"

"He doesn't wear glasses."

"If those aren't glasses, they are the thickest set of contacts I've ever seen."

Seabright stood on her toes to see over the crowd, hoping her French friend would return since too much of the cruise was cruising by without him. Meanwhile, their *bateau mouche* glided a stone's throw from Paris' most impressive monuments. A mocking loneliness clawed at her insides as she once again experienced something special without someone special at her side. The grand galleries of the Louvre appeared then disappeared from view as the Seine split to form a moat around the little island with the big history, Ile de la Cite.

Where is Robespierre? The line for libations couldn't be that long. Maybe he bumped into someone he knows. I hope he doesn't have a woman in every port. This is worse than being alone on top of the Eiffel Tower. Oh no, it looks like we're going to pass Notre Dame before he gets back. How would I ever find him in a city the size of Paris if he suddenly disappeared?

"*Mademoiselle?*" She turned to find her Frenchman had circled around the back of the boat to sneak up on them. In his hands were mini bottles of wine which he first offered James.

James studied his poncho, paunch, and other oddities not to his liking. "No thanks."

"I appreciate your generous gesture," she interjected, clearly embarrassed by her brother's abstinence. "Since you already opened the bottles, I'll help you dispose of his after I dispose of mine. Say, you sound kind of stuffed up. Are you feeling okay, *pere*?"

"Sic et non." He oscillated his hand like a wave on the sea.

She couldn't believe how much his glasses aged him, but his stellar intellect made such disfigurements seem like endearing eccentricities. The poncho was another matter. It had to go, and fast. "What's with the gaping garment? You could hide a corpse under that sartorial tent."

"You're obviously not a wool and wingtips man," James added without a burp of respect.

Robespierre made a gesture under his poncho, seemingly profane.

Not liking that they were not getting along, she snapped the elastic on his poncho. "I should have introduced you earlier. James, this is Robespierre."

The cloaked clergyman held out his gloved hand. *"Enchante."*

James kept his hands in his pockets but nodded. They immediately turned away from each other like magnets whose force fields repelled each other.

Seabright refused to let their mutual repulsion ruin the ride. She rocked back and forth like a toddler at Christmas, tickled pink that she could see the most scenic stretch of the river with Robespierre at her side. Huge spotlights accentuated the deeply-carved facades of famous Right and Left Bank sites, converting each monument into a dramatic three-dimensional *chiaroscuro*, and Notre Dame proved to be the best *chiaroscuro* of all because of its beautifully balanced towers and stone symmetry. Even the irreverent lapsed into an unscheduled bout of homage as the grand cathedral glowed in front of them. A hush passed over all the unwitting worshipers on board, all but Seabright and Robespierre, that is, whose cathedrals had become museums.

James solicited a response from his sister to keep from losing her to the creep. "I like your description of Notre Dame now that I see it up close and personal. The rose windows do look like giant Spirograph designs and the flying buttresses do resemble petrified locust legs."

Seabright was mortified, having assumed that if she put on airs, no one else would take them off her. Instead of breaking the ice, James had fallen right through it.

The French father corrected James with more than a spoonful of condescension. "The locust legs, as you call them, are *arcs-boutants,* but you know this if you are the architecture buff your *soeur* says you are," he added, tossing him a bone to defuse his disapproval.

"Sis, did you know Napolean designed Paris' grand boulevards with triumphal arches to imitate Imperial Rome? Even La Madeleine was modeled after a Greco-Roman temple. It was nicknamed the Parisian Parthenon. Verticality was the signature of power, that's why you see so many spikes, pinnacles, and steeply pitched roofs along the river here."

Seabright couldn't wait to buy postcards of all the places their boat was passing, certain they would make great bookmarks in the advanced literature her priest was providing. "I'd like to hear Robespierre elaborate on the Roman influences in Paris. Like Hemingway said in his hooch-happy novels, I'd love to go to Rome tonight and never come back."

"Then you should jump off the boat up here on Rue Saint Jacques," James continued, trying to draw her away from the dangerous dalliance. "Saint Jacques is the ancient road that led to Rome from the heart of the Latin Quarter. Academics ushered in the Italian influence when the Mansarts croaked, the guys for whom all these curvaceous French roofs are named."

Robespierre did not appreciate the fact that James knew things about Paris that he did not. He had come to hear him confess, not wow Seabright with details that he would have wowed her with, given the time and textbooks. He tried to distract James with a series of sighs and coughs. When this failed, he made a prolonged visit to his pocket watch to insult him with premeditated inattentiveness. Collar or not, he was not without his own ambitions and affections.

James thrived on competition, but he was unaccustomed to such rivalry from a religious man. He embarked upon a recitation of facts, hoping to bring to light the priest's dark side. "The City of Light offers a smorgasbord of religious reliquaries, hand-carved confessionals, ornate altarpieces, lofty naves, sacred statues, and ancient stained glass that rarefy its holy light. Paris is famous for its Gargoyle Gothic, or are churches also anathema to your new theology?"

"Paris' mosques and museums are more charming," Robespierre challenged him.

James fought hard for his sister's attention, not wanting a nut like him attaching itself to their family tree. "Sis, can we do a walking tour tomorrow of Paris' most stunning churches?"

Her face drained of virtue. "Buildings bore me."

"Baroque buildings won't. They're swirly-curly ornate. I call it frosting architecture."

Robespierre kissed the top of her hand. "Staircases can be as sensual as the naked body."

She tugged on his poncho sleeves as if wanting to undress him in front of a watching world. "Father Robespierre is helping me get in touch with my sexuality. *Oui, oui, oui!*"

The Bohemian man of letters untangled two of the more pronounced hairs in his mustache which had been sleeping inside his nose. *"Apres nous le deluge!"*

"After us the flood?" James sizzled though not generally inclined to sizzle. "I don't know French, but I do know French history. You're admitting you're as corrupt as Louis XV."

Seabright leaned against Robespierre. "Never mind him. He thinks he's the Holy Spirit." She cupped her hands to her eyes like binoculars to spy the treasures in the distance. "This is *tres* cool! Why did I ever want to go to Portugal when I could come to Paris? *C'est la vie!*"

"*C'est la mort,* you are not in Kansas any more." He twisted his ring as if it were cutting off the circulation in his finger, spilling his wine in the process.

"I'd love another chalice of cheer, but I don't want you to leave again," she whined.

"Don't look at me to be your carrier pigeon of poison." The American athlete glared at the mustached minister, unable to put his finger on what it was that he disliked so much about him, but knowing it was something, if not everything. "Where is your parish located?"

"The whole world is my parish," he replied as the boat crawled slowly like a barge.

"You didn't answer my question."

He pointed at the Left Bank. "Sainte-Chapelle in the Latin Quarter."

James went over the map of Paris in his mind. "Is it a Christian church?"

He pulled his glasses down his nose. "That depends on your definition of Christian."

"I'm not boarding that train of spiritual derailment with you. Heretics think they are clever semanticists, but God uses their own deception to catch them. God sets good traps."

Robepierre's glasses steamed up, betraying the conniption fit he was trying not to have. "Your brother's religion has made him a suspicious man."

"*Au contraire,* I've always been suspicious of suspicious characters," James countered.

Seabright dragged her brother downwind so the hippie priest couldn't hear. "Robespierre included you tonight out of the goodness of his heart. He's trying to help you."

"He's the one who needs help," James laughed as he did a stand-up push-up on a bench.

"How can you talk that way about a minister?"

"If he's a minister, God is a monster. What kind of pastor hates the Bible? Oh, and Sainte-Chapelle is on this island we're passing to our left. It's *not* in the Latin Quarter."

"You can't possibly know Paris better than a Parisian."

"Sainte-Chapelle was on my architectural itinerary because it has the oldest stained glass in Paris. It's a medieval masterpiece. The filtered light from those fifteen sacred windows tells the story of the Bible from Genesis to the coming Apocalypse in kaleidoscopic color."

"Color my ass. The Bible is as black and white as an eye chart, but not nearly as interesting. I see red from cover to cover like every other slaughterhouse religion."

"You didn't talk this way before you met this minister."

"I was brainwashed by Bible thumpers like you." Seabright stared at the couples strolling the Left Bank, confident she and her suitor would soon be numbered among them. "If you know so much about Sainte-Chapelle, why did you have to ask him if it's a Christian church?"

"I played dumb to lure him into a state of complacency. Liars can't afford to get lazy, or they get tangled in their own yarns. Something is off about him, and off is a scary place to be."

"You thought you could get away with using Socratic Method on a professor?"

"No, I just pretended to be ignorant to expose his ignorance," he said with a wink.

In one glorious moment, the Grand Palais and a royal palace of Louis XIV made their appearances on opposite French shores, one looking as sober as the Supreme Court while the eclectic exhibition gallery was a happy hodgepodge of flying horses and Art Nouveau. Little Red Riding Hood seemed oblivious to the scenery, however, as James' words stuck in her heart like javelins. "McDonalds is a fast food chain, so Sainte-Chapelle could be a church chain. There are many Notre Dames, so there might be many Sainte-Chapelles."

"It's possible, but not probable, sis."

She torpedoed her wine, determined to find pleasure where she thought it should be. "I won't forfeit my hope for your fear. Maybe I want to do something dumb and dangerous."

"Don't we all. The choice is yours, but you can't choose the consequences. I couldn't." He glared at Robespierre who looked ugly and arrogant, perhaps ugly because of his arrogance. *I don't see what she sees in him. Any warm fuzzies he emits must be from farting in his own fat pants.* "I wouldn't be caught dead alone with him if I were you, especially at night."

Her face blanched. "You're scaring me."

"Glad to hear it. This is not a good time for you to die."

"Fear is a pagan construct, much like a *nuit blanche.* Robespierre can explain it to you."

"I don't trust his explanations."

"I'll thank you to let me enjoy the remainder of this cruise without any further input from you, Señor Shot-Put." Seabright spun around on her heel then marched back to Robespierre's side as if mention of Napolean had put her in a military mood. Her sea legs soon left the shore, however, sending her tumbling into his arms like a Vaudeville act in need of a cane.

As the night cruiser looped around the Ile de la Cite, James kept close tabs on his sister, much to her chagrin. He approached her with much prayer and hesitation after the huge watercraft completed its nautical U-turn. "Sis, that fairytale castle with the black towers is the cone-topped Conciergerie, a notorious prison during the French Revolution. Is Robespierre trying to reinstitute the Revolution by making a god out of his opinions?"

Fury spread across her face like a contagious disease. She knew what James was saying was true, but she couldn't believe he had the guts to say it. "We are both fans of the Revolution."

Robespierre kissed his fingertips as the passenger boat kissed the quay alongside the Hotel de Ville. "The Enlightenment was the *Siecle des Lumieres,* the Age of Light.

"Historians believe the French Revolution *ended* the Enlightenment," James rebutted, "and the fruit of your revolution was a Reign of Terror that resulted in 1,400 lob-off lobotomies."

"Nothing cheers one up like a spot o' terror. La Guillotine, known affectionately as the National Razor, actually symbolized regeneration. It superceded the cross, *Monsier* Woodlawn."

"But people discarded the cross when they pinned La Guillotine on their lapels, *Monsier* Monster. The cross *is* light, so nothing is enlightened without it, not even your Enlightenment."

"*C'est comedie noire.* We must instruct through insurrection. *Elever par emeute.*"

"If the revolutionaries were so well instructed, why did they mistake Notre Dame's statues for French kings when they hacked at them in a self-righteous rampage? The favorite pastime of the original Robespierre was beheading. How enlightened is that?"

The bibulous Bohemian covered his ears with his yellow hood as the Eiffel Tower reappeared on the horizon. "*Folie de grandeur.* There is no art in your young heart."

The boat shifted on its fluid host, but James refused to lose his footing. "That's a lie."

"Art cannot lie," Seabright postulated, hoping she sounded enlightened.

"Art can't, but artists can. They do it every day. The architecture of the Enlightenment is delicious, but its ideas are deceiving. Wood was carved to look like drapes, walls were painted to look like scenery, and columns were twisted like twine. To me, Baroque is like frozen theater."

Seabright stepped on James' tenny. "Quit showing off."

"I'm not showing off, I'm showing him up, so you won't be fooled by this Pied Piper."

Smiling like a shark at a scuba seminar, the Frenchman pointed upriver at the glittering landmark with the great iron legs. *"Pardon,* what is that needle *de lumiere* in the distance?"

"You know very well what it is, *faux* teacher," James growled.

"Maybe I play dumb to expose the dumbness of you," the priest replied cagily. "Did I say my church was Sainte-Chapelle? *Lapsus linguae,* slip of my lips. *C'est* Saint Charlemagne."

James turned redder than wine, realizing Robespierre had overheard their conversation. "Charlemagne wasn't a saint and isn't a church."

The colorful man of the cloth dangled his pocketwatch in front of James' face to hypnotize or harass him, whichever came first. "You have not much time before the *bateau mouche* returns to port. You came to tell me about the *meurtre* at *La Tour Eiffel,* no?"

"No, but I hear you were there, so why don't you tell me about it?"

"It is your confession I came to hear, *s'il vous plait.*" He smiled like a used car salesman whose business card read: When life gives you lemons, unload them as lemonade.

James ratcheted his beret back and forth to grind the irritation out of his mind. "The day I confess anything to a spiritual shyster like you is the day I mistake shot-puts for meatballs."

Seabright dragged her brother to the back of the boat again. "Don't blow it for me. It's always been a fantasy of mine to find a father who would abandon his faith for me."

"That selfish, devilish—excuse the redundancy—proposition came from the Pit. The devil births bad ideas in birdbrains who let him. I don't want you to get hurt, not here or hereafter."

She let the breeze catch her hair so that it would lash James across the face. "Nobody's perfect, and I'm not one of those proud people who pretends to be, but this *is* my perfect chance to color outside the lines like a real *artiste.* I might get hurt, but I won't die and go to hell."

"Are you sure about that? There is a killer on the loose, don't forget."

"If I don't forget I don't have any fun." She held her hands out sideways and flexed her legs as if the boat were her surfboard. "Don't rag on me for taking a risk on love, because none other than C.S. Lewis himself said you have to be vulnerable if you are going to love at all."

"God wants us to be hurtable, but He doesn't want us to hurt ourselves. That's as twisted as the staircase in the Louvre pyramid. Love is hypnotic, but it's self-hypnosis. It's something you do to yourself. This guy is a goofball at best and a wolf at worst."

"He has a few flaws, but where's the adventure in cookie cutter relationships? Romance is a vacation for the heart, and I came to Europe for a well-deserved vacation."

James wondered why, of all the Frenchmen in Paris, she had to pick a priest. "It's obvious you've fallen in love with him, but are you willing to fall away just to be with him?"

"I resent the fact that you seem to think I'm going to crash and burn, little brother."

"God might let you crash, so you *don't* burn." He gauged her reaction, allowing for the fact they were floating. "I hope he hasn't asked you to lose the laundry, sis."

"He's a priest so that kind of intimate info belongs in *our* confessional."

James grit his teeth with intense frustration as if he knew any words that would pass between them would fall on deaf ears. "I wouldn't be caught dead inside Notre Dame with him."

"Why?"

"He might just leave you at the altar."

CHAPTER ELEVEN

Poste de Police, Eiffel Tower
10:23 a.m. 24 February

"You would not believe what a priest just told me," announced the ill-tempered old-timer cop who wished ill on everyone who crossed him, everyone who thought about crossing him, and everyone who even looked cross-eyed at him.

"Did he confess to the Eiffel Tower murder?" joked the junior officer.

"No, but a woman confessed to him that she committed the murder."

"Priests are not allowed to divulge that kind of privileged information."

"I guess nobody told this priest that."

The young cop with the marshmallow heart found it difficult to believe the worst about the American girl who toured the tower all by herself. "What is the name of this priest?"

"Gustave Flaubert."

"That's preposterous. Flaubert was a famous French author."

"I guess nobody told this priest that."

Still inexperienced enough to care about his job, the cheerful rookie polished the brim of his can cap with a tissue from the can that was not a cap. "What did this priest look like?"

"A gypsy, but not just any gypsy. He's the gypsy that paid our police post a visit before the corpse even cooled," the geezer growled with a self-satisfied mixture of impatience and impertinence. "He came forward to inform us that this woman showed off her stolen *boules* ball while in line with him for tickets to the tower."

"And what is the name of this woman who supposedly confessed to the murder?"

"Danielle Seabright, but she is using her last name as her first name in France. That is another nail in her coffin. The gypsy priest doesn't know where she lives, but he's been trying to find that out. All he can tell us is that her uncle's apartment is near Montmartre cemetery."

"Hers is the same name the computer spit up from the Civitas Dei yearbook."

"It looks as if we'll be putting the cuffs on her. The priest also turned over her ticket stub from the tower which places her at the Eiffel at the time of the murder."

"Too little is adding up to too much. I feel like a big fat fish being lured by a pound of putrid bait. How is it that all of this evidence ended up in her betrayer's hands?"

"They were drinking, that's how. She showed him the souvenir stub at Brasserie Diable Agneau. However, we must treat her carefully, because her uncle is an attorney here in Paris."

"What is his name?"

"Parker."

"Parker what? Parker Seabright?"

"The priest isn't sure. If we find no address assigned to that name, we should look at the motorcycles near Montmartre cemetery. The girl's uncle lives within view of the plots and rides one of those big American bikes."

"A hog?"

"No, there was no mention of any farm animals."

"A hog is a Harley-Davidson. We'll hear it before we see it."

"Yes, that's the bike. Next question: What do Americans wear these days?"

"Whatever styles we created two years ago, three in the farm states. He may be wearing leather riding pants now that it's winter."

"*Lederhosen?*"

"No, chaps. They're like full-length *lederhosen* with the crotch cut out," explained the biker wannabe. "Only a German American in Paris would wear *lederhosen* on a motorcycle."

"The priest also produced a photo that shows her in an Eiffel Tower photo booth."

"What is a man of the cloth doing at a bar, and is he not a thief himself if he robbed her of her photo, her souvenir ticket stub, and her ability to trust men of the cloth?"

"Your desire for this woman is clouding your ability to see her complicity in the murder. You would rather believe an ugly cleric is guilty than a cute student. However, it is clear to me that we have the evidence we need to throw the book at her."

"First, I want to follow up on the leads we have on this other clean-cut man in the security films who is wearing a wool coat and wingtips. He looks out of place with these young guys, one of whom wears a college jacket and the other of whom wound up dead. He looks British whereas they look American, so I doubt they speak the same language," laughed the happy cop. "Some evidence points to this girl—suspiciously *too* much, however. We can't stick all of our hounds on the wrong scent because we think this creep is going to kill again. Killing is emotional heroine to serials. I'm going to set about trying to i.d. the business face, if you don't mind."

"I don't mind, but I don't help, either," replied the codger cop.

CHAPTER TWELVE

Notre Dame Cathedral, Seine
6:47 p.m. 24 February

Seabright studied the pit-faced demon perched next to her. Its vise-like claws gripped the ledge of venerable Notre Dame Cathedral while its laser eyes zeroed in on its prey 125 feet beneath it. Vicious desire drew its skinned torso into vivid knots as it prepared to pounce on a *bouquinista* far below. A beard dangled from the creature's chin like a severed tongue while its horns and fangs made a cage seem like an appropriate address.

"Aren't you glad the gargoyles are merely petrified personifications of demons, not the real deal?" said Parker while stuffing his riding gloves in his flame-kissed half helmet.

"I don't know if I believe in the real deal any more," Seabright replied as another tour bus dumped its wind-breaking cargo in the square below. "Paris has made me rethink my thinks."

"Has Paris or has this parish priest?"

"Does it matter? Like Twain, I came to Europe to find something thoroughly foreign with nothing that reminds me of anything back home. That's Robespierre, and that's Montmartre."

"At least there are no American fast food franchises in the historic square facing Notre Dame like there now are in Athens' Syntagma Square and Rome's Pantheon Piazza."

Seabright stared at the cathedral's forest of pinnacles and turrets. She wanted to bounce some things off Parker, but she didn't want anything to bounce back that would burst her bubble, hope being such a priceless commodity. To delay the confrontation that she herself had scheduled, she counted the bridges, barges and *bouqinistas* far below the gargoyles.

"The 15th century Seine bridge that led pilgrims to Notre Dame used to have rows of Medieval houses on it much like the Ponte Vecchio in Florence and the Rialto Bridge in Venice," Parker chit-chatted. "The square in front of Notre Dame is called *Kilometre Zero,* the point from which all distances in France are measured. The Bible is my *Kilometre Zero,* the standard by which I measure all sermons, including those with words. When in doubt, I throw it out."

She stared at the scintillating French city through the gaping jaws of a gargoyle. "I used to give out Bibles on birthdays and Halloween, which is probably the devil's birthday, but I've come to realize there's a lot of crap in the Bible. People are better off without it."

"I bet you think you can fly off this belltower right now without getting hurt, too."

"I feel just about that happy, yes. I suppose you have a problem with that, too."

"They say love is temporary insanity, but apostasy is eternal insanity."

"He happens to be more Christlike than Christians. I'm not afraid to sin around him."

"That isn't Christlike. That's Antichrist-like."

Seabright stared across the foreign fantasyland of Paris, wishing she could trade in Parker's company for her priest's. Trying her best to survive the boredom, she peeked inside the belltower proper. "Is this really where the famous Hunchback of Notre Dame hung out?"

"Certainement. Did you know that tale by Victor Hugo helped raise funds to restore this captivating cathedral after the 'enlightened' minds of the French Revolution ravaged it?"

"The church deserved to get sacked. Robespierre said it was doing a brisk business in superstition for the superstupid. It tried to cover the cost of the cathedral by marketing rosaries, indulgences and pilgrimages. Some churches even sent their relics on tour to cash in on 'sacred skeletons.' Why weren't those ecclesiastical episodes carved into its portentous portal?"

"What portentous portal?"

"The main door. Someone seemed to find it necessary to depict people being damned in the carving over that door. Robespierre doesn't think anybody will be damned."

"The Bible calls him a fool, and if he doesn't repent, he's going to be a damned fool," Parker replied. "Your father sounds like a fugitive from the truth, not an apologist for it."

"Don't judge. You don't even know him. Can't you face the fact that religion is an opiate, an oppressive force full of obnoxious opprobrium?" Seabright goaded him.

"What a gross perversion of the truth. Is he perverted himself, perchance? The Church made mistakes, but it's a mistake to judge the Bible by those who misuse it."

"The Bible contradicts itself, that's why Robespierre doesn't believe it."

"No, it contradicts him, that's why he doesn't believe it." Amiable Parker couldn't believe she was losing her faith at the same time that she found herself inside soul-nourishing Notre Dame. "Why does he marginalize Scripture? Does it condemn something he condones?"

"Uncle Logic, I didn't come up here to hear your temptation termination routine."

"Why did you ask me to come up here?" he asked as ribbons of purple and pink unraveled across the evening sky. "Did you want me to ask Quasimodo for his autograph?"

She hesitated for a moment, calculating the damage he might do to her adventure. "I asked you to come up here because I heard these towers are well suited for...torture...and torture is a perfectly lovely way to extract a confession out of someone along the Gallery of the Gargoyles on a vulgar Sunday afternoon." She looked away, afraid of her own admission.

"Is this provocation the product of a dark sense of humor or a dark heart?"

Seabright tried to conceal the darkness in her own heart. "I like his sense of humor."

"I hear a but..."

"But, you don't like him and James doesn't like him."

"Do you like him?"

"You know me. I like everything I shouldn't."

"We all do, hon."

"He's enchanting, almost evil..."

"That's a big but. What's almost evil about him?"

"Almost everything."

Parker studied a gargoyle as if she were describing one. "Is he a friend or a fiend?"

"A misunderstood friend who turns theology on its head to make people use their heads."

"Yours truly never met him, so how do you know I wouldn't like him?"

"You don't like anyone who doesn't like the Bible."

"Oh, this must be that guy from the pub, the one who's pretending to be a pastor."

"Someone ordained him."

"Ordination is no *imprimatur*. Some seminaries are so suspect their pictures belong on post office walls. They'd nominate a gargoyle as a ministerial candidate if they found the premise to be intellectually stimulating enough. Their delight in provocation betrays their pride."

"Whatever. Orthodoxy is a myth and a mythtake. He's dedicated to righting its wrongs."

"I find it hard to believe the Church got it wrong for 2000 years, and turning it upside down will somehow make it right. He sounds like the *Poseidon Adventure* of theology."

She chewed on her cheek to hide a guilty smile. "He's very spiritual in his own way."

"All these buts might be nothing but trouble." The biker's eyes darted about the tower as if he were its proprietor. "Check out Galatians 1:6-9 and run for your life!"

"Why? Because he thinks differently than you do? Most people don't think at all."

"No, because those who preach a different gospel are doomed to be damned."

"Is 'Run for your life!' a popular saying over here? He said the same thing to me."

"James?"

"No, Robespierre."

"He's toying with you, and you might ask yourself why."

"I might ask myself, 'Why not?' He's a fun guy."

Parker tried to picture the large-hipped loser. "He could be the devil incarnate."

"He sure likes to quote the devil a lot," she tee-heed. "He plays the devil's advocate to make people think. Priesting gets to be a drag after hearing so many drag queen's confessions."

They inched their way to a ledge where gargoyles died drooling into a decadent jalapeno dip. "The portentous portal's sculptor included a bishop among the damned."

She sizzled despite her heartfelt frostiness. "What are you implying, Parker?"

"The company you keep portends the trouble you'll meet." He tied his biker bandanna like a pirate, albeit a pirate in *lederhosen*. "I hope you're not planning to see him any time soon."

"Is tomorrow too soon?" she laughed. "He thinks I'll love the Louvre."

Parker listened with his eyes as she spoke. "Mind if I join you?"

"To Robespierre? *Avec plaisir*! That would make me a *fille de joie*."

"A hooker?"

"No, a woman of joy. That's one of Robespierre's nicknames for me."

"That kind of *fille* turns tricks for treats. Satan will turn your treats into tricks. You'll think you're in for the time of your life when you're entering the hour of your death."

"Thanks for the doom 'n' gloom. I didn't get enough of that at Civitas Dei."

"Is it just going to be he and thee at the famous French gallery?"

"I wish. Unfortunately, he wants James to join us."

The Bible biker made a steeple of his fingers. "*Merci,* Master."

"But James won't be coming. He's a guts 'n' guns guy, so I don't want to embarrass Robespierre with his commentary since my professor has an IQ as big as the national budget."

Parker glanced over the side of the tower, hoping to see the Latin Quarter hotel where he stayed on his first trip to Paris. The colorful wisps that decorated the sky had disappeared entirely, making it impossible to distinguish his dive from all the other student dives. "It's a great big world, and I'm glad you're seeing it, but no territory is as treacherous as deception."

"It is a great, big world, and I will see every inch of it *sans* fear. Saint Augustine said, 'A man who knows only his own country is like a man who reads but the first chapter of a book.'"

Parker's aqueous eyes watered in the wind but he thought it would be off-putting if he put on his riding goggles since they were attached to his helmet. "Standing on shifting sand feels like a carnival ride, but the properties of quicksand are quickly understood when that ride ends."

"I'd rather be on a ride that ends than no ride at all," she laughed while letting the wind wrap her hair around her face like a feathery tail around a horse's ass.

Parker's eyes followed another *bateau mouche* as it swam from bridge to bridge in the twilight. He was afraid of the answer but asked the question: "How was your Seine cruise?"

"James and Robespierre didn't hit it off."

"Why did James tag along?"

"It was Robespierre's idea. I can't wait to melt in the statuary of his arms."

Parker arched his eyebrows. "How does Robespierre know James?"

"He doesn't. He heard about James' complicity in the murder and wanted to help."

"Help how?"

"He agreed to hear his confession," she announced, eager to put the incident behind her. "Robespierre was at the Eiffel Tower the night of the murder and saw everything."

"Everything? What everything?"

"I don't remember. I'll have to check the tape. My Frenchman has been recording our conversations. He says so many memorable things that I can't write them down fast enough."

"You didn't say anything implicative about James, did you?"

Seabright did an about-face just about in his face. "It's none of your business what I say or to whom I say it. You don't have the right to tell me what to do."

"I'm trying to look out for both of you while you're staying with me in Paris."

"I won't be staying for long." The gargoyles gave her the creeps, but she didn't admit it because she knew it was indicative of her guilt. However, it felt as if they were coming to life just to occasion her death. "I hate this stupid wire netting up here. Why do churches find it necessary to cage us in even when we're outside? I guess God never met a cage He didn't like."

"It's a safety net. Left to our own devices, we'd all jump off one ledge or another. God is no Cosmic Killjoy. 'No good thing will he withhold from those who walk uprightly.'"

She tried to enjoy the panoramic view of Paris despite a foreground of foreboding creatures. "Speaking of hookers, did the Revolution enshrine a hooker goddess in Notre Dame?"

"Yes, and that should tell you everything you need to know about the French Revolution. They turned this delicate sanctuary into a godless Temple of Reason, 'reason' that resulted in mob rule. Revolutionaries held a mock funeral for the Church. Cartoons depict the clergy hanging from lampposts. They also converted the Pantheon into a tomb for terribles like the original Robespierre. Another dreadful moment in noble Notre Dame came when Napolean the Narcissist chucked the pope in the clink so that he could crown his own proud self king."

"Pride is a good thing. Robespierre says pride is the soil in which our talents grow."

"He pancaked that point. Pride is the manure in which all our *sins* grow."

"God said He'll give me the desires of my heart, ergo, copulation is copacetic."

"That's as twisted as a noodle, but people who think they have sharp noodles often feel entitled to rewrite Holy Writ. Your clerical quack is cloaking his heresy in the verbiage of erudition, so you'll think he's a 'misunderstood intellectual,' but he's as deluded as Louis XIV."

"You're a font of foreboding. I trust him more than I trust you right now."

Parker had a chilling sensation the killer was watching them from some turret across the Seine. "James is better with buildings than I am, but I know this ledge between the balconies is called the Gallery of Chimeras. Did you learn about chimeras in Greek mythology?"

She felt like pushing him over the edge. "A chimera refers to wild fantasies that demons can turn into dashed dreams, but I didn't come here to have my dreams dashed."

"Notre Dame is a dream come true for many craftsmen, but it took 170 years to build, so they had to invest their lives in a holy task that they knew they would never get to see completed." A rack of floodlights began to drown the 30-foot rose window in white light.

"I'm not comfortable standing out here since the lights came on," said Seabright. "Notre Dame is just another morality play writ large, intent upon making me feel guilty. Even La Madeleine's classical facade had to go and carve the Last Judgment into its stupid frieze."

"Most Parisian passers-by pass right by the Judgment, but a seventeen foot Messiah is hard to miss. Blaise Pascal wrote, 'God so regulates the knowledge of Himself that He has given signs of Himself, visible to those who seek Him and not to those who seek Him not.' God not only wrote stuff in stone, he drew stuff in stone, too. We are all without excuse. Romans 1."

"James calls architecture 'theology writ large,' but he sees God in everything now."

"All great art has a spiritual content, because transcendence is what conveys significance upon the temporal," said the motorcycle missionary. "Art is the apotheosis of imagination, so inspired art is a wink of what is to come. It takes you to places where words won't go."

"I didn't know you were such a thinker, Parker. You're mildly articulate."

"Shucks, it aint nuttin', honeypie. I just take note of the art on my travels, especially the sacred art. Art adds a dimension to my faith not found on the printed page."

"Robespierre is introducing me to truths not found on the printed page."

Parker hung his head but bit his tongue. "That statue in the square below us is the father of Europe, Charlemagne. Folks were illiterate in the Middle Ages, but Charlemagne bejeweled the Bible's covers to let them know the message inside had eternal significance. Art was the Bible of the illiterate, but the value of sacred art is often overlooked today."

"I wish I couldn't read. I just read an inscription that said: 'Let terror appall all those bound by earthly sins.' It was accompanied by a sea of serpents gnawing on the damned."

"God says, 'If you do what is evil, be afraid.' A good scare is better than good advice."

She cocked her jaw to fire back: "But what *is* evil? That's what my pastor would say."

"That says a lot about him." He brushed some salt out of his salt-and-pepper beard. "Did you know the original Robespierre also undermined the Bible while pretending to elucidate it?"

"No, but thanks for asking. I don't fear anything when I'm with him, not even God."

"Did you read *Pilgrim's Progress* at Civitas Dei? Bunyan penned this clarion caveat: 'There is no grace where there is no fear of God.'" Pigeons descended on the north tower like a squadron of albino bats. Lacking bat radar, however, they did their duty where no plumbing existed. "I sowed some wild oats once upon a time, thinking God wouldn't get His girdle in a bundle over it, but the harvest was as bitter as death. Have you ever tasted death?"

"No, but thanks for asking."

"It's beyond any pain you can imagine," he continued, sensing her death was closer than she could imagine. "I held my big, beautiful dog in my arms all night long when he died, running my hands through his fur and remembering all the good times I had with him at the beach, but eventually his body grew stiff and cold, then came the..."

"Undertaker, I hope."

"No, an unbelievable stench that would make Miss Manners hurl."

"Is there a moral to this story?" she demanded, wanting to re-enter the nightlife below.

"Death stinks, but sin is what brought death into the world, so sin stinks, too. The plans the devil has for your life stink. The plans the devil has for your afterlife *really* stink. On the other hand, God has gorgeous plans for you, fragrant plans to prosper and not to harm you, plans packed with pleasant surprises. But you have to be blessable. Check out Jeremiah 29:11."

"Are you quite finished talking about death and stink?"

"No. When I finally had to bury my big, furry friend, I realized the extent to which God is the Giver of Life whereas the devil steals life any way he can. I'm done with disobedience, because disobedience leads to death. All of the devil's doors lead to death."

"What on earth was I thinking when I asked you to climb this stupid tower with me?"

"You asked me to come up here because you have grave misgivings about a priest who twists Scripture like licorice. Can we warm up in the sanctuary below? You want to take in all the art you can, and Notre Dame has enough holy art to reignite anyone's cold faith."

She thought a night visit might be a good chance to daydream of her sinfully romantic plans. "I'll melt my chills, but once my buns get baking, I'm booking."

Seabright rocked back in her little wooden church chair. Notre Dame's soaring verticality made her want to believe in a God that got decked out in stained glass, but she knew Robespierre would mock such things. Savoring the smell of the melting candles and incense, she wrapped her arm over her eyes, content to spend the night if reality would not interrupt her. Before she could drift into an otherworldly oblivion, however, her veins began pulsating with an unquenchable craving as if some creature had made its home beneath the surface of her flesh. "I have to go *now*. There is something at Saint Severin I have to see," she announced.

Parker could smell death in the air, and he feared it had descended on the wings of a false teacher. "What does this something you want to see look like?"

She locked her eyes shut to concentrate on the creature's features. When she opened them, Parker saw two figures darting across her irises. "It looks like one of the gargoyles we saw up on the belltower, except its hideous visage looks like a wolf frozen inside a wind tunnel. Does Saint Severin have gargoyles that look like that?"

He nodded, not liking what he was hearing. "I'd love to visit Saint Severin with you during daylight hours, but I bet it's as locked up as a bank on Christmas now. The locals call the cool columns their palm tree grove, and it has great 15th century stained glass."

"The art is not what is drawing me. The creature is on a roof, and some force is emanating from it with terrific spiritual velocity. Parker, I can see things I never used to see and hear things I never used to hear. Smoke-like shapes float in front of my eyes as if I'm tuned into new frequencies. Its good-creepy like the moonlight in Montmartre Cemetery."

"If creepy feels good, something bad is inside you."

"Bad is a state of mind. I crave that graveyard after experiencing it with a sentient soul. I can see why you took an apartment across from it. Robespierre wants to visit your view."

"I'm sure I don't appreciate that cemetery for the same reason Robespierre does." Parker stared at Notre Dame's high altar and vaulted nave, wishing his good God would keep the bad at bay. "You two didn't call down any spirits of the dead or anything, did you?"

"Technically, nothing is living or dead; it only looks that way."

"That's a bad mix of Buddhism, Hinduism, and New Age nutism. I suspect this creepy pastor is the devil's own. I would get away from him if I were you."

"He's a man of God, and God is love, so I'm sure God is glad I'm in love with him. Look, I no longer choose to subject myself to such bigotry as you espouse. I'm leaving."

Parker prayed for help, knowing there was plenty of help waiting in the wings with big wings. "The Latin Quarter makes the best hot-pressed baguette blends you'll ever taste. Can I tempt you with a low-cal lovely like tomato topped with feta? My treat."

"I don't trust your treats any more. They're beginning to feel like tricks, but thanks for the temptation. I will use your proposition as precedent to proposition my priest."

"Everything that was black is white to you now, but that's not surprising. Plato said anything that deceives produces a magical enchantment. I hate that about earth. It's as if there's a magnetic field at our feet and metal in our hearts that always drags us toward evil."

"I want to get as close to *pere's* magnetic field as I can without crossing over into it."

"To 'cross over' means to 'croak' in witchcraft parlance, and you might cross over if you trample over the cross." Parker handed her a souvenir bulletin from a Notre Dame concert.

"Your scare tactics won't work on me." Seabright drew her hair behind her ears to hear better, not realizing Parker was hearing nothing at all. "Something is waiting for me under the pinnacles of Saint Severin's." She lifted herself off the seat with both hands like a gymnast, then she launched herself into the aisle like a zombie on a mission.

Parker followed her out of Notre Dame's numinous sanctuary and into the darkness. He ducked behind a green *bouquinista's* box along the Seine to see what she was up to, or what someone else was up to. The caped collegian did not pause to look at the lights dotting the river as she crossed Pont au Double, leading Parker to believe she was rendezvousing with the rapscallion named Robespierre. A short time later she marched up Saint Severin's steps as if she'd attended the 13th century *eglise* her whole life, causing Parker some consternation since he knew from their conversation she didn't even know that Saint Severin was on the Left Bank.

Two men were lingering outside the wrought iron fence that wrapped itself around the Gothic House of God like a metal afghan, but neither man looked as if he belonged in the Latin Quarter. One man, formally attired in a business suit, turned his back to Seabright when he saw her coming while the other man didn't seem to realize she was there. Much to Parker's surprise, it appeared as if his determined niece had come to see the man in the wool coat and wingtips, not a priest in pantaloons. The oblivious second man bore some resemblance to James, although he looked thirty pounds paunchier in an artist's poncho.

Seabright stopped dead in her tracks, not because of either of the men but because of the dreadful gargoyles lurking behind her. They stuck straight out the side of the church like vicious battering rams. Each looked like a wolf frozen in a wind tunnel such as she'd seen while in a trance inside Notre Dame. Noticing a man who looked like a portly rendition of her brother caused her body to break out in a cold sweat as if it were trying to shake off a spell that had come over her quite against her will.

She stepped into the shadows of a market kiosk, suddenly full of fear. As she combed through her change to find the necessary funds for a liquid anesthetic, she realized Parker had followed her across the river. "Am I supposed to think it's a coincidence that your riding boots brought you to this side of the Seine absent your ride?" she confronted him testily.

"I'm worried about you. It's pretty late for a pretty woman like you to be lolly-gagging around the Latin Quarter. What are you doing over here?"

"I have no idea," she laughed, no longer surfing on the danger.

"I believe you." Parker looked over his shoulder when he heard footsteps behind him, but both men had disappeared, and neither was ever close enough for a positive identification. "I don't like this. I don't like this one bit. I better give you a ride home," he all but insisted as he offered her his flame-kissed helmet which he purchased to remind him to steer clear of anything that would lead into the forever flameland of hell.

Feeling enough fear to make the offer seem attractive, Seabright replied, "Can we drift around the Left Bank and listen to the accordions and saxophones for a while first?"

"I don't know if that's such a good idea. The Big Bad Wolf plays a saxophone in cartoons, Little Red Riding Hood."

"Don't call me Little Red Riding Hood. I hate that."

"Sorry. Let me take you on a midnight ride up the Champs Elysees. We'll circle the colorful eddy of the Etoile, then we'll zip around the Egyptian obelisk in the Place de la Concorde where the fountain is still trying to wash away the blood from the other Robespierre's razor."

She knew she better go with him. "Okay. Just don't remind me of our conversation in the morning. I don't want to worry about what I'm doing until I'm ready to stop doing it."

CHAPTER THIRTEEN

The Louvre Museum, Paris
9:40 a.m. 25 February

"This just goes to show you that Christianity ought to be one big party," said Robespierre while kneeling before an immense canvas in the Louvre called *The Marriage at Cana.*

Seabright didn't have a clue as to why he was kneeling, but she joined him on the floor just the same, confident his posture enabled him to hear and see things others couldn't. "I have never seen a canvas as big as a movie screen, but can Veronese's perspective be trusted after he painted himself with prominence in the picture while tucking Christ behind a table?"

"*Au contraire.* Art alone can be trusted. It only is pure. You can trust me, of course, but I would not call myself pure *tout a fait.*" He rubbed his belly to acknowledge his appetites.

"You're plenty pure. It's not your fault the Church brands you impure. As for the purity of this painting, classical architecture should not be in ancient Israel, Greek gods should not dwarf Christ, and Jesus should not be portrayed with jesters, jugglers, and jugs of jolly juice."

"That's where you are wrong, my pretty." He patted her on the head as if she were wonderfully naive and he held the keys to her enlightenment. However, his enlightened self soon toppled on his enlightened butt, because he had the rump of a Rubens and the balance of Picasso.

"But you said nothing is wrong, right?"

"Wrong. Ethics is an evolving species, *cherie.*" He assumed a yoga position to convey a sense of his own importance. "You should not say that anything should not be in a painting."

Seabright had never met a guru, but neither did she think she was meeting one now. "It's right for you to say something is wrong but wrong for me to say something is wrong?"

"That is a priest's prerogative: to teach and not to learn." He waited to see if she would call his hypocrisy into question, but Paris was working its magic on her. "Veronese transposed this Bible legend into 16th century Venice because he realized art is not history. Neither is art science. Art is life, and when you understand life, you will understand art."

Little Red Riding Hood felt she had to sign up for more sins to prove she understood anything. She genuflected playfully as if conceding that art were a religion that needed no Bible.

He wrapped his leg over his neck and ripped one. "I believe it was a bishop who said debauchery is a spiritual virtue for the artist because it keeps him from worse temptations."

Her eyes popped with excitement as if she'd just laid eyes on her first Greek sculpture of a Greek athlete *sans* a Greek uniform. "What bishop said that, pray tell?"

He smiled, not wanting to tell her Bishop was the man's last name. "Who cares?" he said, leading her to believe what she wanted to believe which amounted to leading her on. "The French Impressionist Degas wrote, 'Only when he no longer knows what he is doing does the painter do good things.' *Voila!* Only when we no longer care about right and wrong do we do right."

"That's so profound it sounds heretical. Are you recording all this for me?"

"*Certainement!* One never knows when a confession might leap from one's lips." The priest-professor led wide-eyed Seabright down the Denon Wing so that she could enjoy being disappointed by the dark little painting called *The Mona Lisa.*

"Show me someone who appreciates *The Mona Lisa,* and I'll show you someone who doesn't appreciate good art," she snickered, though she had just mistaken Saint Sebastian for a salesman who rang William Tell's bell one too many times. "However, I do like that headless statue with the big wings at the top of the staircase. It is *tres* proud and independent, like us."

Smiling mischievously, he modeled his proud independence by sashaying down the grand corridor, but the model he looked most like was a drag queen, a queen that had been dragged through the streets of Paris en route to her first annual beheading. "That marble figure from the prow of a Greek ship is the *Victory of Samothrace*, but Nike isn't naked, so I doubt it would make your uncle squirm. Let's send mister stiff-and-stodgy a postcard of voluptuous Venus."

"He's really not stiff or stodgy. He's probably rollerblading out in the courtyard as we speak. We had a blast on his bike last night, zipping around the winding lanes of Montmartre."

"Sorry to hear it. Tame James is a bit of a stuffed shift, and I do so enjoy pissing off old stuffies when I'm a bit pissyboots. Shall I pop a nudie in the post for him? What is his address?"

"Same as mine."

"*Oui*, but what is yours? An outhouse in Omaha? I have pen in hand, do I not?"

"I don't remember Parker's address. You get rather bossy when you're stone cold sober."

"Thank God that doesn't happen too often." He picked a flower off his laurel diadem and placed it between his teeth like a Spanish dancer with ears for castanets. "There's a bar in here."

"I'll drink to that," Seabright laughed.

"You'll drink to anything." Robespierre stuck the flower over his ear like a pencil. "I like to meditate on the art quotes they put on the bar's placemats before I embark on a visual visit of the museum. The printed word enhances my understanding of the unprintable."

"It's just the opposite for Parker, art enhances his understanding of the printed word."

The freethinking father plugged his nose to demonstrate his smoldering contempt for the Bible biker. "*Ecrasez l'infame!* You doubt there is a lounge in the Louvre? There is not only a drinking depot but a moat, an auditorium, bookshops restaurants, and a drawbridge."

"There is a drawbridge in a museum?"

"*Oui*, it is from the fortress of Philippe Auguste. The Louvre is an interactive history lesson that you walk through. You should have brought your history buff brother today."

"He'd think you were the devil himself if he saw you partying for *petit dejeuner*."

"I could teach him a thing or two about architecture." Robespierre pushed her toward the stately window as if he were resurrected royalty. "See how the Louvre is *tres novantique*, both medieval and modern? The old part was originally a hunting lodge, and later a castle. Now a new glass pyramid radiates positive pyramid energy into our galleries via the entry pavilion."

"Speaking of old, those Coke bottle bottom glasses you wore on the boat yesterday didn't do you justice, and why did you wear rain raiment when the sky wasn't even spitting on us?"

"The street cleaner splashed poodle poo in my eye, damaging my contacts. As for the poncho, I knew if I looked as irresistibly handsome as I felt, James would suspect us of an *amourette*." His lips touched her ear while whispering the tempting translation. "A love affair."

She had not considered such a wonderful explanation. "If you were trying to look squeaky clean yesterday, why did you wait until today to shave off your mustache?"

He ran his fingers across his face in search of human fur. "Why did you say nothing until now, *cherie*? Do you not prefer me to be clean-shaven in these hairy circumstances?"

"If the clean-shaven are dirty-minded, I do." She thought her candor was noble, even if her sentiments were somewhat ignoble. "To regard the flesh as filthy is a Hindu thing, isn't it?"

"All religion is the same: guilt and offering plates. To hell with it. *Ecrasez l'infame!*"

"You can't say that. You're a priest," she laughed out loud.

"Thanks for reminding me. But there really is no need to define anything as sinful."

She didn't know if he was joking. "If nothing is a sin, then why did Jesus have to die?"

"He created his own reality. Modern minds have since evolved into higher states of consciousness that don't necessitate the shedding of blood. If men shed blood nowadays, it is for the sport of it," replied the Bible-hating Bible teacher.

The unlikely pair strolled through the Salle Sully, peeking at the glass pyramid in the courtyard whenever a window permitted. Next the unorthodox pulpiteer led her to the *Venus de Milo* statue set in a niche of elegant red marble. The guidebook described the work as the prototype for feminine beauty, but Seabright didn't know if Robespierre regarded the work as the prototype for feminine beauty, so she didn't know if she should imitate it or ridicule it to endear herself to him, having not yet endeared herself to herself enough not to care what he thought.

The progressive pastor suddenly spun on his boot heel and announced, "It is most troubling for me to tell you this, but I saw James talking to Hawk on *Rive Gauche* last night."

"I thought I saw a bloated version of him myself, but I also saw a bad ass in a business suit who was the spitting imagine of Hawk, if not Hawk himself, so I didn't get close enough to find out for sure. I couldn't forget a face like Hawk's even though I only saw him for a moment on the night of the murder. Do you think Hawk is the grifter-drifter I loaned my Civitas Dei pen to at the Eiffel Tower, the pen that wound up in the leg of the victim?"

"*Oui,* he is the dashing gentleman of the evening who cruises the tours soliciting funds for his favorite charity: himself. Do you think Hawk saw you?"

"I'm afraid he did, but I wasn't afraid at the time. I'm not afraid when I drink, unlike after I drink when I realize what I did while I was drinking. Something came over me last night besides the brews, or perhaps because of them. It tried to lift me out of my body."

"Out of your body and into my arms?" The Epicurean European posed like a marble goddess who had marbles for brain cells, though he held his head high with cold dignity.

"I don't understand what happened. I was entirely content sitting inside the sanctuary of Notre Dame at the time with my feet propped on a little wooden chair. The ambiance was surreal, and the French hymns sounded like the anthems of angels. With eyes closed, I was savoring the smell of burning candles and incense when suddenly I started seeing these faces of creatures in torment. I felt such hatred for Parker, too. I wanted to spit on him."

"Growing pains, these are just growing pains, *cherie*. It is difficult to break out of the dark prison your beliefs have kept you in," he reassured her while squeezing her neck gently.

"If we really did see James who only looked portly on account of the poncho, what on earth would he be talking to Hawk about? They're from opposite ledges of the universe."

"One might be purchasing an alibi from the other."

"But neither has an alibi if they were both at the Eiffel the night of the murder." She covered her eyes with her arm again, not wanting another day to be ruined with talk of a murder she thought she had nothing to do with. "I'll talk to James about it, but he's as straight and narrow as an arrow now that he repented of his putative carnality, so there's no way he did it."

"Maybe he got scared straight *after* doing it, *cherie*." He curtsied to crack her up, but museumgoers mistook him for a crackpot who had done some crack or pot.

"You don't know my brother, father. He's such a coward, he won't even wear white after Labor Day, not even white undies. I thought I saw James outside a cool Gothic church wrapped up in wrought iron fencing called Saint Severin's. Where did you think you saw him?"

"The same place. I followed him out of the Sorbonne. He was talking to a guy in a wool coat and wingtips, possibly Hawk. Did you know James went to the Sorbonne looking for *me*?"

"Why would he do that?" she gasped.

"*S'il vous plait*, he is checking up on me, no?"

Seabright boiled in her own skin like a lobster in a pot. "I don't know what's got into him, but Parker thinks I'm the one that something has gotten into. Go figure, Frenchie!"

"They are persecuting you, *cherie*. Follow your heart. Your heart is art."

"But it's wired to some bad stuff. I don't trust my heart as far as I can throw it."

"Feelings are fickle, but feelings are our friends." He made the sign of the cross over her heart. "Your heart is your *atelier.* Go there and paint your own truth."

They meandered around the museum's crowded corridors, but the American didn't coo over everything the Europeans chose to put on their walls. Many paintings were too swampy, dark and full of death when she was trying to have the time of her life. Turning a blind eye to the masterpieces whose frames seemed to be more of a work of art than the art itself, she confessed, "I need a change of scenery. This sacred art is yanking at my chains. Why would someone paint a picture of Mary Magdalene petting a skull, and who is so obsessed with death that he designs a sculpture of Jesus on the cross *sans* the cross?"

"Jesus without the cross is the new Christianity, *cherie*!"

"But Christianity *is* the cross, is it not?"

"*Sic et non.*" He touched his finger to her forehead as if blessing her new thoughts.

She wished he would show her something erotic to take her mind off death, but she didn't want to come right out and ask. "El Greco's deep, dark crucifix was too creepy for words."

"If you don't take a fancy to God's dreadful state of affairs, I rather think the next work I shall introduce to you won't be all beer and skittles for you, either, love." The goofy pastor led her to the Louvre's ground floor via the Richelieu Wing, then he waited for her eyes to fall on a series of life-size statues that formed a macabre funeral procession carved out of stone.

"Black-hooded mourners carrying a corpse is not the party Paris should be." She shivered while imagining her own hooded cape turning black as her body rotted in a grave. "I don't know why you're showing this to me. It's as morbid as Parker's cemetery apartment."

He backed up a step, his baubles backing up with him. "What are you afraid of, *cherie*?"

"Hell, of course."

"Did I not tell you, we are all going to ascend to heaven eventually?"

"And I'm supposed to just take your word for it?"

"Would you take the word of a French author? Andre Gide wrote, 'Wisdom begins where the fear of God ends.' But if I believed in hell the way you do, and lived the way you do, I guess I would be afraid, so maybe you should be."

"How capricious is that? Is truth a cafeteria where picking something makes it true?"

"*In vino veritas!* You need a drink. Intoxicants enhance one's spiritual understanding."

Seabright didn't want to doubt him. "You take pride in being different, don't you?"

"Pride is my middle name. Robespierre is a *nom de plume* for 'rebellion.'" He stood like a two-legged Eiffel Tower. "I know pseudonyms can serve a purpose, as do you."

✠

"You're right, drinking puts life in proper perspective. Death is the furthest thing from my mind." She lined her overpriced empties in a row. "A pastor has undermined my faith, making me easy prey for the killer. Whodathunkit? Parker warned this would happen."

"Why let Parker control you? Do you see any killers lounging about the Louvre?"

"No, but there *is* a killer out there somewhere. Let's run off to the Riviera together!"

His nostrils flared like French horns. "The Church would set about defrocking me."

"It should have done that a long time ago." She burst out laughing, causing some bubbling Beaujolais to exit her nose like a polluted fountain.

"I should take you home. Write down your address in case you pass out again."

"What do you mean, *again*? I don't always enjoy your psychotic humor. Parker told me not to let Satan serve as my matchmaker because he joins you to a Judas every time."

"*Bouche cousue!* What brought on that outburst, pray tell?"

"*In vino veritas*." She tiptoed her hand towards his. "Wouldn't you like to squeeze my hand, so you'll know you're the kind of man who enjoys squeezing a woman's hand?"

His eyes took on a haunted look, but he didn't punish her for his pain. "I am a Judas because I choose to maintain a certain level of decorum as a priest? *Sacre bleu!*" He fingered his stubble as if missing his mustache. "Do you expect me to jump up and kiss you in public?"

"*Oui*, a French kiss would be nice," she teased. "After all, we are in France."

"You've had too much to drink."

"Don't fulminate about what you furnished." She drank with spite, and a little spit, as he stuck a toothpick in his Jack-o-lantern teeth so she wouldn't contemplate kissing him in public without paying a price for it. Seabright stared out the great museum window at all the art that had not yet made its way on to canvases. "Why is a brilliant Parisian professor hanging out with a strapped American student?" she backpeddled, realizing she was pushing him too hard.

"Every spiritual pro does some *pro bono* work." His smirk was as undecipherable as water. "But I do have a class to teach, so it's time I took you home, *cherie*."

"It feels like you're trying to get rid of me." She bit her lip to keep from crying. "I looked up the English equivalent for bedroom. Is *chambre a coucher* one word or three?"

"It is two words: not now." He rolled up an art placemat for her to take home.

She loosened the drawstring on her blouse. "*A bon chien* something or other. A good dog never gets a good bone. You taught me that French phrase at Brasserie Diable Agneau, remember? Then we turned it into a song at the cemetery. However, your hypocrisy is now in evidence. After successfully undermining my faith, you aren't going to act on the disrobed result, the denuded *denouement.* At least buy me one last drink to drown my sorrows."

Robespierre sniffed the stuff under his fingernails. "Okay."

She couldn't believe her good fortune. "You will? Life just got better in *bonbon* Paris!"

"I figure you'll let me do anything after another drink, including take you home."

She drew her hair across her eyes like a curtain across a shattered window. "First, tell me which artists' quotes on this placemat elevate you into ethereal realms of enlightenment."

He circled a quote with his laurel centerpiece. "'The artist disturbs, upsets, enlightens, and opens ways for a better understanding. Where those who are not artists are trying to close the book, he opens it and shows there are still more pages possible.' Robert Henri."

"You like that quote because it makes your rebellion sound like art," she chuckled.

Not enjoying her line of questioning while finding it useful to pretend as if he were enjoying it, he turned the tables on her. "Are you attacking the call on my life?"

"My intent was to insult, incense, and infuriate you, but I can see how you might perceive that as an attack," she laughed, hoping to return to the Louvre after reading some books about it.

Robespierre studied a few of the faces in the room. "What does your uncle look like?"

"A German American dressed in leathers, *lederhosen*, and a flaming brain bucket."

"I had a feeling someone was following us. I hoped it was your uncle, not Hawk."

"I know I'm safe as long as I'm with you. I just hope the cops aren't following us."

"You're more concerned about the police than the Eiffel Tower killer?"

"No, but I'm more concerned about the police than Parker. As for the killer, what are the odds that he would pick me to pop out of all the people in Paris? French cops, on the other hand, have good surveillance, so they might have a visual record of my borrowing that *boules* ball."

"They would not follow you into the Louvre two days later for a boy's toy."

"That's a relief."

"Unless of course you murdered someone with it."

"Would I be so stupid as to whack someone with a ball with the whole world watching?"

"You were stupid enough to steal it with me watching."

"I didn't even know the guy. Besides, if I were going to kill someone, I'd poison him."

"Me too." The Pied Piper priest circled words by Oscar Wilde this time. "'A subject that is beautiful in itself gives no suggestion to the artist. It lacks imperfection.' Seabright, God is not offended by our peccadillos and perversions. I rather think they endear us to Him."

"I could justify any sin using that logic, but you don't even believe in sin."

"Perhaps you have not the capacity to plumb the depths of my spiritual understanding."

"Do I need a submarine to understand your theology? If I do, maybe it's all wet," she laughed like a hyena just to hurt him since she felt rather hurt herself.

He leaned their forks together to form an Eiffel Tower. "My theology cannot be reduced to words, so I dip my brush in abstract paint to help you understand what cannot be understood."

"I must have had too much to drink, because that sounds like a bag of bulging balderdash. Have you considered running for office?" She held the salt shaker to his mouth like a mike.

"I'm too busy running from the law to run for office," he howled like a wolf that was enjoying a mid-life catharsis. His emotional enema ended, however, when he read the disgust in her eyes. Fear he found quite delightful, but disgust was another matter entirely.

Seabright didn't want her plans interrupted by reality. "Why would the law want you?"

"Why does anyone want anyone? I have done nothing wrong."

"Is that because you redefined 'wrong?'" she cackled.

A vein in his temple throbbed as if preparing to burst. "Your simplistic notions about right and wrong are an insult to intelligence everywhere. There is no need for you to criticize what you do not yet comprehend. Like Socrates, I have been accused of corrupting the youthful elite, but the established order is a constipated lot that loves to suppress those with zeal and unzippered jeans." He circled Picasso's quote that was as scrambled as his works of art. "'Painting is a blind man's profession. He paints not what he sees, but what he feels.' My theology is what I *feel.*"

"Is theology that fluid? Is nothing fixed? Monet loved water so much that he wanted to be buried in a buoy, but even a buoy has an anchor. It is both fluid *and* fixed."

He ratcheted the bones in his neck as if determined to snap his spine. In two.

"*Pere*, Paris is foreign to me. It isn't easy to cross over into your frontier of faith."

He straightened his knickers and leggings to demonstrate his *bienseance* civility, assuming such civility would lend credence to his new teachings. "James also attended Civitas Dei, did he not? Perhaps the charming lad can explain my theology to you."

"I'm sick of talking about James. I'd like to mail his tail to Timbuktu."

"But he might be the murderer and that would mean your uncle is harboring a fugitive."

"I told you, if James killed someone, I'm sure it was an accident."

"Most accidents are on purpose," Robespierre laughed.

CHAPTER FOURTEEN

Holiday Hotel, Montmartre
3:20 p.m. 26 February

Seabright tossed a musty pillow from the forties into a dusty window from the thirties. The 1730's. "Why do I have to stay in this sour suite? I might be spending the night on Montmartre, but this dive has no bar and no balcony, and I'll have to take a shuttle to the can."

"Would you rather be spending the night in jail? This no-tell hotel may be a pit, but the French are too passionate to be fascinated by good housekeeping." James locked the door that did not want to lock. "Did you realize someone paid the police a visit, and that someone told them a story whose ending makes you sound like the Eiffel Tower killer?"

"That theory is so lame it needs a telethon to support it."

"The cops are looking into it, and they're looking for you."

Her eyebrows betrayed her shock. "Does Parker know they're looking for me?"

"He'll know soon enough. That's why I got you this room. If the police find you at Parker's, Parker would probably lose his license to practice law for harboring a fugitive."

"That's just what Robespierre said, but I don't want that to happen, because that would make him a motorcycle missionary 24-7, and the planet can't handle that much theological imperialism." She threw her book bag on the fake Louis the XIV furniture which had been designed by Louis the XIVIIXI, the owner's grandson. "I'm going back to the Eiffel Tower incognito to hunt for my *boules* ball. If I find it, that will clear me and my conscience. It's probably lodged in the webbing between levels one and two, but Robespierre thinks it could have plummeted to the ground like a cheese wheel chucked from a French Alp."

"That's something else I want to talk to you about."

"Okay, I admit I borrowed the glorified marble from a jerk at Parc Chien."

"I meant Robespierre. I need to talk to you about that twit in the tights." James realized there would be no room service, and it looked as if there had been no maid service since the French Revolution. "Are you telling me you also stole that *boules* ball?"

"Also? What makes you think I borrowed anything else?"

"A newspaper report said you stole some cheese from a *fromagerie*."

"It's not my fault the cheesehead wouldn't take my chump change. I offered to cut the cheese, but a customer had already done just that, judging by the smell in that brie boutique. There's only one way to settle this: I'm going back to the tower to find my *boules* ball."

"Are you kidding? That place is swarming with cops, and the Eiffel Tower's cameras have already visited your face. Did you take a picture of yourself in a souvenir photo booth?"

"They have security cameras in the photo booths, too?" Seabright gasped.

"No. The tipster-tattler turned in a souvenir picture of you from a photo booth along with a ticket stub that places you at the scene of the murder at the time of the murder."

"You read all this in the paper?"

"Yes."

"Then Robespierre probably read it, too. That must be why he's been acting so weird, weirder than normal. Why didn't you bring the paper so I could see the stupid article?"

"I thought I might set it down and forget about it, then someone else would see it and the cuffs would be slapped on you before you had time to take the shuttle to the poo shed."

"Oh goody. How did you manage to get this room up here on Montmartre?"

"It's a no-show. Someone pre-paid the tab stateside after reading about it in a travel guide, but she said the write up was a work of fiction when she saw the room for herself."

She hugged a pillow as if it were Robespierre but refrained from planting a kiss on the cotton, knowing it could turn into cotton balls before her eyes. "You said you wanted to talk to me about my priest? I know he's a bit of a loose canon, but it's not as if he has loose morals. He has no morals," she laughed, confident that all concern with immorality was a sign of immaturity.

"That explains why he bought you so many drinks at the Louvre."

Seabright threw the pillow at him. "How did you know?"

"I followed you. But before we get into that, I want to give you this." James reached inside his peacoat on loan from Parker and pulled out a laminated card. "Since your butt seems to be backsliding into brimstone, I brought you another temptation termination card."

"I'd rather choke on a gourmet goose than wreck my romance by reading that."

"You might become a dead duck if you don't wake up. Your life is in danger."

"In danger of not having any fun!" She poked her head out the old French window like a restless puppy in a room full of new toys and old shoes.

"Hawk is trying to frame you or kill you, probably both," James explained. "If you don't take the fall for the Eiffel Tower murder, he might just toss you from the top of it."

"Uncle Parker said the tower is no longer tossable since they fenced it in."

"A lot has happened in Paris that shouldn't have happened." James double-checked the door lock then sat on a bed. It broke. "Please hear these Scriptures before the cock crows?"

"Must you be so melodramatic?" She gazed out the ratty lace curtains to see if anyone was following them. "Robespierre thought he saw you talking to Hawk. What's up with that?"

"Hawk has been blackmailing me, so I won't testify about what I saw at the Eiffel Tower."

"The devil's disciple can't blackmail someone who has done no black deeds."

"I let him talk me into drinking with him, then he took advantage of it," James lamented.

"He who? Hawk or the devil?"

"Hawk *is* the devil incarnate."

"Whatever. Buying off a blackmailer always backfires. Just put a stop to it, fraidy-cat."

"I can't. He threatened to kill you if I did. He's not blackmailing me for bucks."

"Then what is he using as blackmail bait, pray tell?"

"Your life. My silence has purchased your safety for the time being."

"But you weren't silent. You tipped off the cops."

James nodded reluctantly. "I did so anonymously before he went into the blackmailing business, Danielle...I mean 'Seabright.' Do you think Hawk knows about that?"

"How would I know? I haven't seen hide nor hair of him since the night of the murder."

"That's what you think."

"You can't count the time I supposedly saw him while passed out up on Montmartre."

"You spoke with him on the Seine, as well."

"No, you were the one who was seen talking to Hawk by the Seine, not me."

"I didn't say *by* the Seine, I said you spoke with Hawk *on* the Seine."

"Hawk was on our *bateau mouche*? Why didn't you warn me?" Seabright yelped.

"I didn't know it was Hawk until those waves were in our rear view mirror."

She sniffed the wallpaper, wondering in which century it began to decompose and whether something had decomposed behind it long before that. "Why is Hawk out to get *me*?"

"I don't know, but if he gets you, I take the fall for the Eiffel Tower murder, sis."

"I thought you said he framed me, not you."

"He framed both of us. One of us is an insurance policy."

"So, that's why you're still wearing that shaveable camouflage and artsy-fartsy beret."

"Like I told you at Chez Chateau, Hawk managed to get my fingerprints on the *boules* ball and the wine bottle, he tricked me into planting false evidence in full view of the Eiffel Tower cop shop, and he took pictures of me with the victim at some dumb vineyard we visited."

"Pray tell, how does that implicate *moi*?" she replied, as self-absorbed as a sponge.

"Our Christmas picture from Cape Hatteras was found in the victim's wallet."

"But I didn't even know the victim, so why would Hawk want to frame me?"

"Evil is its own inspiration, and Hawk is pure evil. His eyes are like ice balls."

Seabright stared out the window at the winding cobble lanes of Montmartre, never thinking a dream could come true on the same day that a nightmare did. "Let me see if I've got this straight. Hawk asked you to meet him on the Left Bank, then he agreed not to kill me?"

"He was letting me know I better not rat him out or he would rub you out. Your life is worth more to me than his capture, but it's an imperfect arrangement since I know he could strike again. At least I told the cops all I could. I suspect he planned to kill me that night, too."

"Why didn't he?"

"You and Parker arrived unannounced on the scene, so he exited, stage left."

"Blackmail is one thing, murder is something else entirely."

"Not if you've done it before. Sin twice and it doesn't feel like sin. He had a strange bag with him, and I doubt it was full of groceries. I suspect it was his kill bag. I tailed him for a while, but tailing ain't easy when you are a target yourself."

"How did he contact you? Does he know where you live? Why aren't you dead?"

"He left a message for me at the Rue Danton gym where I worked out one day for a week," James joked. "Hawk hangs out by the Sorbonne. That's where we met at a French class."

"My priest could have taught it! Maybe I can figure out Hawk's real name from the student roster. Robespierre warned me about Hawk. He said he cruises the tours looking for suckers to fleece. When you ran into him, did you get the feeling he wanted to kill you?"

"No, kiss me."

"Come again?"

James looked away, clearly embarrassed. "He came on to me the night of the murder. He hit on the guy he killed, too. That's another reason why I think I'm next on his hit list."

"Robespierre explained Hawk's m.o., not his motive. Do you think Hawk could have murdered that guy from your French class because he rejected his advances?"

"Maybe. He's a control freak, one of those proper types that's as anal as underwear. His victim laughed at him. Laughing at people probably hurts more than killing them."

"Brotherboy, what makes you think Hawk doesn't know where you live?"

"I'm not dead, am I?"

Seabright opened and closed the closet, wondering if Hawk was planning on coming out of one. "This dive doesn't even have a phone. We couldn't call for help if we had to."

"If we called for help, we'd have to do what help says."

"Spare me the lecture or I'll hit the nearest libations line."

James tested the lock again then read aloud from the new temptation termination card. "'Not everyone who says to me, 'Lord, Lord' will enter the kingdom of heaven.'"

"Goats don't get in. I know that, at least I knew that," she snickered while combing her long black locks. "As a matter of fact, I told Robespierre about that verse in the cemetery."

"Did he respond with an eruption of goat gas?"

"He didn't agree, but he's French, so what do you expect? I don't want to go there now."

"Then we're going there later. I'm worried about you." James finally saw the advertised view of Sacre Couer out the window...the bathroom window, that is, after taping a mirror to a hanger. "The first warning reads: 'The wolf catches the sheep that separates from the flock.'"

"What a coincidence. Robespierre said the same thing to me up here on Montmartre."

"There are no coincidences in a Christian's life."

"Did I say I was a Christian?" Seabright sizzled, itching to abandon him.

"We're reading this not a moment too soon. Your temptations could lead to your final termination. What if the Eiffel killer slit your throat as you were eating an egg salad sandwich?"

"I don't eat egg salad sandwiches, but thanks for thinking of me."

"Verse number two, sis: 'Be sober.' I Thessalonians 5:8."

"*C'est impossible*. Only a fool would be sober in Paris."

"Only a fool wouldn't be, especially with a killer on the loose, a killer with whom you've had personal contact. Feed the flesh, and the flesh will eat you alive, so says the Bible."

"Not everything is in the Bible."

"Not everything isn't. Coincidentally," he teased, tongue firmly in cheek, "the next warning reads: 'If you believe what you like in the Gospel, and reject what you like, it is not the Gospel you believe, but yourself.' Saint Augustine said that."

"I don't care if Saint Paul said that. That's just another gratuitous slap at Robespierre."

"Parker didn't know Robespierre when he made these temptation termination cards. God knew him, however." James dropped a few euros in the coin-operated fireplace, fearing his toothpaste might freeze into a peppermint stick. "Scripture three: 'If, in spite of this, you do not listen to Me...I will punish you sevenfold for your sins.' Romans 7:13."

"You wonder why I loathe Christianity? Who can love a God who loves to punish pew potatoes? A religion predicated upon a cosmic case of child abuse is devilish."

"Funky fiddlesticks. Something's gotten into you. This pastor has twisted you, sis."

"That's what Parker said."

"'Funky fiddlesticks?'"

"No, he thinks something has gotten into me. He thinks I can't see the forest for the trees, but I think maybe we are the forest and the trees. Temptation is the last frontier."

James spun around to face the door as muffled footsteps traversed the hall way, but the feet continued climbing to a level two levels above them. "'One who has known the way but turns away from the Lord will receive greater condemnation. If they have escaped the corruption of the world by knowing our Lord and Savior Jesus Christ and are again entangled in it and overcome, they are worse off at the end.' II Peter 2:20."

Seabright knelt on the floor, but not to pray. She saw another pair of shoes pass under the door, and she was quite willing to pee her pants if those shoes were wingtips.

"One last loving warning," said James. 'The devil turns away from a closed door.'"

"The devil incarnate might be outside our door," she whispered on bended knee.

He knelt beside her. "Robespierre isn't teaching a class this morning?"

"Very funny." She slid James' mirror device under the door.

"Like Parker says, the Bible will keep you from sin, and sin will keep you from the Bible. 'If anyone turns a deaf ear to the law, even his prayers are an abomination.' Proverbs 28:9."

"I define prayer differently now, and I haven't opened my Bible since I got here."

The mirror caught on the hinge, so James reached for the door knob instead.

Seabright leapt to her feet. "Where are you going? Parker said you can get locked inside these old hotel rooms if one person leaves and the other doesn't."

"I'm taking the shuttle to the can. Don't worry, the devil can't get in unless you let him in." James turned the archaic brass key. "How can you get locked inside your own room?"

"You can't lock the door on the outside without locking me in on the inside. There's no independent interior release on these humiliating old haciendas, little brother."

"I have something important to tell you, but I must pee. Why don't you come with me?"

"Not to the john, James, but neither am I going to waste my night in Montmartre trapped inside this odorous dive. Europe at its finest is right outside that door."

"Can we have a chat with Europe's finest when I come back?"

"Not if my life depended on it."

"Your life might, and so might mine. We have to talk the minute I get back."

"I won't be here when you get back."

"Oh yes, you will be." James locked the door behind him.

CHAPTER FIFTEEN

Parker's apartment, Montmartre
3:20 p.m. 26 February

Parker tripped over his flipper slippers as he answered the door in his Harley sweatpants and John 3:16 jersey that had John 3:19 printed in French on the backside for backsliders. He wasn't expecting anyone, but he was always praying for people to cross his path whom the cross could help, so he was never that surprised when the doorbell bonged. "What can I do for you?" he asked the oddball visitor dressed in pantaloons, pantyhose, and a pink blouse.

"Does James live here?"

"Who are you?"

"Who is any of us?" The stranger turned his head to sneeze but didn't remove his gloves to blow his nose. "I am the king of the forest, I am I am, and you shall be my queen."

Parker hoped he was another Nicodemus at night but didn't offer any info about James.

CHAPTER SIXTEEN

Poste de Police, Eiffel Tower
3:20 p.m. 26 February

"We have two more sightings of Little Red Riding Hood," boasted the obstreperous old cop as if he had gambled on her guilt just to make his job more interesting. "What did you find out when you staked out her uncle's cemetery apartment?"

"Her uncle lives on his motorcycle. He bikes to breakfast, bikes to work, bikes to play, and gives out biker Bibles along the way. I do not think he is harboring our fugitive."

"Which fugitive? Danielle Seabright, the coy thief with the flowing black hair?"

"Little Red Riding Hood may be young and foolish but that does not make her a fugitive," replied the young and foolish officer. "I have news about the spick-and-span businessman in the wool coat and wingtips whom our surveillance cameras recorded at the tower the night of the murder. I also have some news on that flowery gypsy priest who paid our cop shop a visit."

He raised an eyebrow with an air of disbelief. "What is this news?"

"They come and go from the same address."

CHAPTER SEVENTEEN

Place du Tertre, Montmarte
5:30 p.m. 26 February

Seabright dipped four carefully chosen French fries into a tub of tartar sauce, not wanting to waste drink calories on food since she hoped to go pub crawling as soon as her priest crawled onto the scene. "That's laughable! How could you possibly think Robespierre and Hawk are the same person? It must be a brother thing. Brothers are often jealous of sisters' boyfriends."

James canvassed the artist's square, furious that she insisted on eating at one of Paris' most popular tourist haunts when the specter of a killer still haunted them. "Why do you think I asked him point-blank on the Seine cruise if he was a wool and wingtips man?"

"That's the dumbest thing I ever heard. You're just jealous."

"Please finish that fry so we can go back to the room, sis. This is dumb and dangerous."

"Tourists flock here to fulfill their dreams, so Place du Tertre is covered with undercover cops. Besides, I acquiesced to donning your artist's poncho, so Hawk won't recognize me."

"What about Robespierre, his evil twin?" he asked, investigating the irony.

"FYI, Robespierre happens to be a hairy Bohemian who looks like a Bolshevik ballerina while Hawk is a clean-shaven businessman whose business consists of conning coach potatoes."

"They both say *Wizard of Oz* lines, and they both say *sic et non.*"

Seabright threw a fry at him. "That makes Robespierre the Eiffel Tower killer?"

"Why do you think I've been following him? Where do you think he went when he disembarked the *bateau mouche*? Rue de L' Universite. He has an apartment up by the Eiffel."

"That's no crime. It's a crime that I don't have an apartment by the Eiffel Tower."

"I've also been following Hawk. Where do you think he lives?"

"In a fiery furnace full of fiends?"

"No. Rue de L' Universite. He lives in Robespierre's apartment building."

"They come and go from the same building, and you assume they're the same person?"

"Robespierre said *c'est la mort* on the *bateau mouche*. That's what Hawk wrote on the suicide note at the Eiffel Tower. *C'est la vie* is a famous phrase meaning 'It is life!' *C'est la mort* is obviously a *jeu de mots*, a play on words that he made up to mean something like, 'It is death!' Your priest isn't fluent in French, so how could he possibly teach it?"

"He teaches English as a second language, not French."

"He probably said that to cover his tracks. I bet English is his native tongue." He kept a watchful eye on those who were watching him. "The papers said he fled England for France."

She stopped chewing, remembering his frequent use of British slang. "A serial killer fled England for France, not a Paris priest. When you assume, you make an 'ass' out of 'u' not 'me.'"

James tossed his napkin at her. "I bet he thinks he can outsmart the cops. That would explain why he's hanging around town when most killers would cruise. He's toying with us."

"I can't believe my ears! Robespierre can't be a serial killer! He's a minister, not a monster! Picture them side-by-side. Robespierre has an eyebrow ring; Hawk doesn't."

"Hawk is the type of guy who would pierce his own skin for the fun of it, so the fact that he removes his eyebrow ring to become Robespierre is no surprise. I saw him puncture a dead man's thigh with a Civitas Dei pen, the one you gave him, I suspect," James explained.

"You think I gave my pen to Robespierre, not Hawk, the night of the murder?"

"Robespierre *is* Hawk. I highly doubt that anybody else from Civitas Dei was on the tower that night to give him one of our school pens. By the way, why does Robespierre wear a ring? Priests don't wear rings unless they're married, and if they're married, they're not priests."

"He's married to God," she snorted. "It's none of your bee's wax, but that ring belonged to his sister. She got run over while rollerblading down Boul' Mich. Does Hawk wear a ring?"

"He wasn't wearing one the night of the murder, but he wears one now, and I have a sick feeling it belonged to the victim. Serial killers often take trophies from their victims." James gave a few coins to a Montmartre beggar who went from heat lamp to heat lamp looking for a handout. "You said he's a professor at the Sorbonne, but I checked and no Professor Robespierre works there. I doubt a university of that caliber teaches English as a second language, either."

"Keep your nose where it belongs." Seabright poured her French swill down her throat though it tasted like tub water.

"Sis, it's not as if I expected to find Hawk while following Robespierre."

"What are you saying?"

"Robespierre went into a gay bar by the Sorbonne; Hawk came out."

"That proves they're *not* the same person!"

"*Au contraire*. Robespierre was in there long enough to have changed clothes, not to mention identities." James continued to circle the square with his eyes, afraid one of the artists might not be an artist, though the modern art made suspects out of most of its creators.

"Now you're accusing my priest of being a wolf in sheep's clothing?"

"Why do you think he twists Scripture with a passion? His passions are twisted."

Seabright stormed inside the *brasserie* and slammed another glass of foam as the happy colors of Montmartre melted before her eyes. Stumbling back outside, she bummed a smoke from an artist who was obviously bummed about something, judging from his self-portrait of a janitor who was self-medicating by self-administering a swirlie.

James gave her some time to let the news gel in her mind, but he knew it might never gel in her heart. She bided her time blowing smoke at him, although most of it blew back on her. At long last she whimpered, "Do you have any more temptation termination cards?"

"I thought you'd never ask." He pulled one out of his velcro 'n' vinyl sports wallet.

"Don't think I'm buying into your black-and-white worldview. I'm just so angry that I need to distract myself with something that will make me even angrier. Change channels, Tame James. I don't want to hear another idiotic accusation about Robespierre." The cigarette nipped her fingers before napping on her lap. "I want to buy something just so I can break it!"

He handed her a level four temptation termination card then read the Russian proverb on it that Russian Cossacks probably ignored while drinking themselves blind in the artists' colony. "'What the Devil brings he also takes away.' That's an incentive to intercept iniquity."

"Oh goody. More flame-filled foreboding." She snatched the card from him. "'The Lord has departed from you and become your enemy.' I Samuel 28:16. What a stupid coincidence. Robespierre said the same thing to me while we were sitting up here in Place du Tertre."

"The Lord can speak to us even through our enemies."

"Robespierre is not my enemy."

"A friend who leads you astray *is* an enemy. Ezekiel the watchman gave us this warning as medicine for our immortality: 'When a righteous man turns from his righteousness and commits iniquity...he shall die in his sin. The righteous things he did will not be remembered.'"

She blew her cheeks out. "Why are there more Bible verses than quotes on this card?"

"The Bible says it best." James rocked back in his chair to see who was seated behind them. "The best place to hide might be out in the open. Maybe Hawk won't look for us where we shouldn't be. It could be safer out here with a hundred witnesses."

"A hundred witnesses didn't stop him at the Eiffel—it turned him on. On the other hand, Robespierre likes to hang out in happy Montmartre, so he might show up at any time."

"That's why you insisted on coming out here, isn't it." James could not fathom her stubborn stupidity. "Love affairs make fools of us all, but deception is a more deadly affair."

"If he's 'married to God,' it's not technically an affair, right?"

"It's wrong no matter how you look at it, unless you're standing on your head. Your shoes seem to be firmly planted on the ceiling ever since you met him. I fear you've bought a portrait of the spiritual world from an artist whose perspective is as warped as Picasso's."

Seabright knew she couldn't possibly drink enough to erase James' ceiling shoes remark. Worse yet, she knew drinking had probably contributed to the flight of her feet. "It can't be safe holed up in that hellhole without a phone. I'll finish reading this stupid temptation termination card if you'll let me hang out here until that dog artist signs her painting with a paw print."

"Deal. Proverbs 1:25 reads: 'Since you rejected Me and you ignored all My advice, I will mock when calamity overtakes you like a storm.'"

"That's dreadfully negative, James." She peeked out her poncho to see if Robespierre was cruising the cobblestones. "The next verse for a hearse is Amos 4:12, 'Prepare to meet your God.' This is just the kind of dumb distraction I need, but skip the scream theme in Luke 12."

"No. 'God said unto him, Thou fool! This night thy soul shall be required of thee.'"

She stared at the stale liquid that smelled like the last thing she threw up. "This tastes awful, smells awful, and is an awful waste of calories, but I feel awfully good for a little while if I can keep it down," she laughed as if she wanted to cry. She plugged her nose so she could finish the foamy fluid. "My man of the cloth can't be a murderer. Some sexually twisted people in the clergy might think they're getting away with murder, but that's a far cry from real murder."

"Not so far that God can't hear it, Seabright. If he's flaming now, he's going to be flaming later. That's my pithy paraphrase of Jude 7 and I Corinthians 6:9, sis."

She stared at a breadstalk the size of a baseball bat, wondering if the lack of preservatives could transform it into a real baseball bat by morning so that she could fend off the killer, or James, whichever proved to be more of a problem. "Robespierre has a broom mustache whereas Hawk is as baby-faced as a banker. They can't *possibly* be the same guy."

"You said this priest is also an actor, so don't you think he has access to a costume closet?" James hoped his five o'clock shadow was starting to look more like a mustache. "Serial killers are good actors, or they wouldn't be able to leave a series of bodies in their wake."

"He's not a serial anything so shut up with your rabid speculations."

James rolled his eyes while sipping his nourishing *citron presse*. "Hebrews 10:26-27 says, 'If we keep on sinning after we have received the truth, no sacrifice for sins is left, but only a fearful expectation of judgment and of raging fire that will consume the enemies of God.'"

"Oh goody, more fear and negativity. Nietzsche was right about you right-wing religious relics. The true enemies of our spiritual evolvement are you unenlightened pew potatoes."

"Chapter and verse, *s'il vous plait*?" James asked pointedly.

"I'll let you know the chapter and verse after I write my own Bible," she replied equally as pointedly. "Do you think these stupid temptation termination cards are prophetic?"

"Why do you ask?"

She splashed her throat with another swig of swill. "Every card is too coincidental. Too often, someone has said the same thing to me that I just read on one of Parker's cards. They've served to spoil my fun, some of which I remember."

"What fun? Backsliders don't have any fun. Their guilt goes with them everywhere they go. How can you enjoy waterskiing on a lake where boating is forbidden when you know it's forbidden because its currents will plunge your butt over a dam? Backsliding is like spitting into the wind, and spit only tastes good when you're too drunk to tell spit from spaghetti."

She stared at her artist poncho disguise. "Even if it is a sin, I won't go to hell."

"That's a novel way to go about your business," James voiced his concern with so many vowels and consonants. "For what fleeting sin are you willing to risk an eternity in hell?"

"None of your business. Everyone sins every day, so why worry about any one sin?"

"Premeditated sin can put a sinner in very hot water: water called the Lake of Fire."

She recoiled like a snake. "Shakespeare said, 'To do a great right do a little wrong.'"

"Just because Shakespeare said something doesn't make it true. Scripture tells us to do right or we might be left behind. Look up Luke 17. God might dump your derriere into a devil's cauldron to get you to repent. Check out I Corinthians 5:5. God does wake-up calls."

"I don't accept long distance calls from strangers. The last pitiful platitude from party pooping Parker reads: 'When you start serving Satan, he doesn't tell you he's going to throw you away when he's done using you.' That reminds me of a tune I just heard down in the Metro as if Satan himself were hiding in one of the subway tunnels. When Judas' sin catches up with him, he howls, 'Just don't say I'm damned for all time!'"

An artist in Place du Tertre popped open his easel as if smitten with a sudden burst of inspiration. He dipped his *cerise* croissant in orange paint, tipped his canvas horizontally, then let the flakes topple like a shower of autumn leaves on to its wet surface. The result was a painting as textual as a Van Gogh, though likely to be modified by future applications of bicycloheptene dicarboximide for bug infestation.

"Sorry to break it to you," James added, "but I thought of something else that Hawk and Robespierre have in common. Neither looks as if he's darkened a dentist's door."

"Teeth like a train wreck?"

"Exactly."

"That's how Robespierre described Hawk's teeth." Seabright sucked on a French fry to make it last as long as a real meal while thinking out loud. "But the fact that Robespierre warned me about Hawk proves they're not the same person. Would you talk in a vividly unflattering way about a third party if you were that third party?"

"I would if I were trying to deceive the party I was partying with."

She stared at the miniature ball and chain necklace on a nearby tourist. Her conscience transmogrified it into a miniature *boules* ball. "Does Robespierre realize you suspect him?"

"He knows I'm trying my best to make his life miserable, but I don't know if he knows that I know, you know? Pride makes people feel invincible." He turned his head sideways to read the time on her wrist clock. "Like it or not, it's time to check in with Parker. He stuck his neck out for us, so I won't let Robespierre drop a guillotine on his neck."

✠

James plugged his right ear so he could hear what Parker was saying into his left. "Did you say Robespierre came to your apartment?"

Seabright seized the phone from him. "Was he looking for me?" she panted.

"He was looking for both of you," Parker replied, "but he left a message for James."

"James?" Her hair stood on end. "Nothing for me?"

Parker turned the envelope over in his hands. "No, this is addressed to James."

She dangled the phone by its cord like a rat by its tail. James retrieved the vocal instrument from his dazed sister. "Parker, both the police and Robespierre are watching your place, so it's not safe for me to come over and get the meathead's mystery message."

"I'll come to you instead. That meathead can't keep up with my panhead." Parker exchanged his sweatpants for *lederhosen*. "He's sitting in the cemetery even as we speak."

"There's a carousel at the bottom of Sacre Coeur. Can you get there?"

"In a heartbeat. What color camouflage are you sporting today, James?"

"You'll recognize your peacoat on yours truly, and Seabright is wearing my artist's poncho that can put thirty pounds on you if you let it, not that she'll let it, of course."

Parker looked below to make sure Robespierre was still in the cemetery. He wasn't.

CHAPTER EIGHTEEN

Sacre Coeur, Montmartre
7:12 p.m. 26 February

"Parker isn't taking his own safety into consideration, sis," James lamented while they waited for him below the snowy white domes of Sacre Coeur in Square Willette.

"He knows Paris better than we do and he's heavenbound, so why worry?" she replied.

"Your selfishness is as mind-boggling as your new theology." A posse of horses paid them a visit courtesy of a colorful carousel, but no killer had saddled any of the plastic stallions.

Soon a metal stallion roared on scene. Seabright dashed into the open to confront Parker the moment his motorcycle stopped purring. "What was Robespierre doing at your apartment?"

"Looking for you two. He took a visual inventory of the surroundings before leaving this envelope for James." Parker used the hedge as camouflage. "He left his gloves on while blowing his nose. That's unnatural. Equally weird was the way he looked up and down the hall when he left, then he went and camped out on a cemetery bench, of all places."

James opened the envelope. "He might be hiding out in the open like we did."

"Hiding from what? Heresy hunters? The CIA, Clergy Impostors Anonymous."

"No, the cops. Robespierre is Hawk," James announced through gritted teeth.

"He is not," Seabright protested, her face as flat as a coffin lid. "Hawk is as cold and mechanical as an ice machine; Robespierre is as hot and unpredictable as a hurricane. Hawk is as hairless as an albino rat; Robespierre is as hairy as a bear. Robespierre is totally disarming."

"He's disarming because he's trying to disarm you, sis."

"Help me put two and two together," Parker requested. "How are these two alike?"

"Robespierre the flaming heretic and Hawk the icy businessman come and go from the same apartment building by the Eiffel Tower; they both have teeth like a train wreck; they both speak fluent English and a little British English but next to no French, and they both quote lines from the *Wizard of Oz.* No Professor Robespierre teaches at the Sorbonne, and the *coup de grace* is that Robespierre went into a gay bar and Hawk came out," James added like frosting on his cake. "Hawk has been trying to find me since the night of the murder, and Robespierre has been using Seabright to try to find me since the night of the murder."

Parker studied the buffet of bodies around him, but no entree was as fruity as the priest who paid him a visit. "That's amazing but not the least bit amusing. Neither can I say I'm surprised. Pastors who subvert Scripture are doing the devil's work on earth, and the devil kills everything he can get his hands on...or somebody else's hands on."

James glanced over his shoulder then read the message. "The man with two faces says he wants me to meet him on the south tower of Notre Dame along the Gallery of the Gargoyles."

Seabright latched on to his arm. "Don't do it."

"Why?"

"Because..." she began, afraid to spell it out for him, "it could be dangerous."

Parker ratted out the priest *avec plaisir*. "He told her the Gallery of the Gargoyles is a perfectly lovely place to torture a confession out of someone on a vulgar Sunday afternoon."

James' eyes grew wide as wheels. "We're all in danger because I didn't come forward when I should have, so I'm going to do whatever I have to do to get us out of this."

Seabright was so dumbfounded, she felt dumb for the first time in her life. *The brother I dissed is willing to die for me?* "I'm going with you. I'll prove he's innocent. There isn't a bad bone in his body. He's reduced his entire religion to: 'Love and do what thou wilt.'"

"Any priest who thinks he can correct God's Word is full of the devil."

"You two aren't going up there without me," Parker put his foot down. "Seabright and I will already have climbed the 387 steps to Gargoyleville by the time this vampire rises from his coffin. When James and Hawk arrive, Hawk won't realize we've been up there for hours."

"Stop calling him Hawk." She feared the ways in which the plan and her heart might fail.

Parker popped his half helmet on a passing horse for a ride around the track to see if any onlookers would jump the decoy. They didn't. "We'll have to study the floor plan and hope there's a secret passageway to the tower from the sanctuary. We'll send James into the tourist square at *Kilometre Zero* bright and early so that Hawk's beady little buzzard eyes are focused on him as we sneak into the tower from some passageway inside the Notre Dame, *Deo volente*."

"Is Quasi Modo going to escort us through this secret passageway?" Seabright sneered as the horses seemed to dump all over her dreams.

The carousel started up unexpectedly again. "If God can make a way in the wilderness, He can make a way through one of His houses. It may be unorthodox, but so was Rahab."

"So is Robespierre. That's the only reason you suspect him."

✠

"This is torture," Seabright protested while staring out the hotel window. "Memorable Montmartre is all around me, but I'm trapped in this dirty dive like a rat in a sewer. I take that back. Sewers might be a shade better. At least they're wet. This *auberge* is as dry as a Baptist wedding. I'm stone-cold sober *and* scared to death, pardon the redundancy."

"And well you should be," said James while studying the design of Notre Dame.

"Well I should be sober, or well I should be scared out of my mind?"

"Both."

She unzipped her book bag to display the fruit of her newfound knowledge. "Your narrow interpretation of the cross, the Bible, and the world are ruining everything for me."

"Those ceiling shoes must be a very good fit. You're still talking like a passenger on the *Poseidon Adventure*, thinking Robespierre is going to turn the world right side up after all of Christendom didn't notice it had it upside down for 2,000 years."

She scuffed her way to the bed where Parker was looking for secret passageways on an architect's drawing of Notre Dame. "How did Robespierre find your apartment?"

The motorcycle missionary blinked with disbelief. "You didn't tell him where I live?"

"I made a point *not* to tell him."

"Why?"

"Because he made such a point of asking."

Parker resisted the temptation to make tea out of that which the tea leaves were clearly telling him. "When was the last time you saw Robespierre?"

She hesitated, not wanting to surrender the secrecy which made each rendezvous so much fun. "We toured the Louvre yesterday. He's teaching me how to color outside the lines."

"And live outside the lines, no doubt," James peeped. "I know he didn't follow you home because I followed you home, but he's probably been watching Parker's apartment from the graveyard. Did you leave Parker's place at any time last night?"

"I ran to the corner kiosk for a cold Kronenburg around 9."

"Parker let you enter the night near piggy Pigalle unaccompanied?"

"No, I came and went while he was in the shower."

"Is Robespierre familiar with the corner kiosk in question?"

"*Certainement*. That's where we reloaded."

"Reloaded what?"

"Ourselves. We got loaded all over again after running dry in the cemetery. It sounds bad now but felt good then. I hoped I'd run into Robespierre while making a beer run."

"He probably stalked you from the kiosk back to Parker's place. Ironically, you snuck out to meet him, but he didn't even let you know he was there watching you the whole time. He followed you home instead. There's a good chance you led the killer right to us."

"Stop it. You're scaring me."

Parker held up a poster of Notre Dame, comparing it to an interior diagram. "One false move on the tower tomorrow and we all might exit earth and enter eternity. James, you know architecture better than I do. Can you see some detail that Hawk might overlook?"

"He'll overlook plenty since he doesn't know Paris any better than a first year French student. He didn't even know Sainte-Chapelle is on the same island as Notre Dame."

"But Hawk may see things we don't when he dials up the devil for disaster relief. We have to be covered with prayer if we're going to have a prayer of a chance at catching him."

Seabright stared longingly at the mansard roofs, clay pot chimneys, Old World lanterns, winding lanes, and wrought iron balconies outside their Montmartre window. "Call the cops if you really think he's the killer. I don't want to go to hell before I've seen Athens and Rome."

Parker kept one finger on the map's enlargement of Ile de la Cite. "Don't you think you should do something to change the possibility that you might go to hell tomorrow? There are no exits in the Abyss, and the more you continue to sin, the less you'll be able to stop sinning."

"If I hit the brakes, the ride is over."

"If you hit a wall, your nightmare has just begun."

"I'll take my chances."

James felt as if he were talking to an occult cultist, but he knew what a potent narcotic sin had been in his own life. "No cops. We have to play by Hawk's rules, or he might kill you."

"And you," Seabright countered competitively, not wanting to be the only one that bought the farm if it suddenly went on sale.

"He likes to kiss people before he kills them, so it's obvious that he deliberately deceives people. It's only fair that we deceive that deceiver."

"*Sic et non,*" Parker replied. "Deceivers deceive themselves. Besides, vengeance belongs to the Lord. God sets good traps. You'll be the one to trip if you set the trap."

Seabright chewed on the inside of her lip, her only source of protein that day. "We better be careful or we might step in one of God's traps by accident."

"If you step in God's trap, it's no accident."

CHAPTER NINETEEN

Notre Dame Cathedral, Paris
8:48 p.m. 27 February

The City of Light succumbed to darkness once again, but the urban landscape kept itself awake with a scintillating array of lights–reckless concatenations of red taillights winding their way up the Left Bank of the Seine, streams of white headlights zipping down the Right Bank, nervous neon jumping around the jazz clubs of the Latin Quarter, party lights dancing atop the floating *vedettes*, and stately skyscrapers casting a pinkish glow across the narrow garden of water. French monuments and churches that looked flat and gray by day sprang to life with warm, romantic hues of saffron and coral at night. Spires and towers, barely visible against the bright blue of the day sky, stood out like spears of lightning against the black backdrop of sundown. Even the glass pyramid of the Louvre changed color as it filled with fiery amber light.

James was not as attentive to the architectural highlights of Paris as he wanted to be, however, since he found himself tiptoing across the stone ledge that looked down on the Stygian metropolis from the staggering heights of Notre Dame. To calm himself, he breathed rhythmically as if preparing for an athletic event, or the end of all his athletic events.

The voices of tourists mingling about the square below him stood out in stark contrast to the haunting quiet behind him. He didn't want to leave the balcony to climb up the last section of the tower because he knew its steps were even steeper and its niches even darker. Neither did he want to find himself any farther from the safety of the crowd below. *Hawk told me to meet him on the Gallery of Gargoyles. So, where is he? Then again, why do I expect a killer to keep his word? God only knows where he's hiding on a dark night like this. For all I know, he could be looking down at me through one of the scopes on top of the Eiffel Tower.*

Knowing he wasn't even supposed to be on the tower, the athlete crept across the narrow ledge that clung to the cathedral in an attempt to look for Hawk one last time before bailing on his plan. Then he heard it, the sound of someone jumping on to the stone gallery behind him. He spun around but saw no one. "Who's there? Who is it?"

Footsteps shuffled across the dark double niche, but James knew Parker or Seabright would have answered him had the shuffle belonged to them. As he moved toward the disturbing disquiet in the south tower, he heard something new in the north tower. Trying to remain calm in the company of his predator, James baited him, "I can see why you waited for the tourists to leave the scene." His voice was deliberately nonchalant like the recorded message on an answering machine. He tiptoed a little farther down the dark ledge as the murderer tiptoed after him. "It wouldn't have been much fun killing me in front of the clicking cameras of tourists."

"That is exactly the kind of fun I fancy," Hawk laughed in a tone suitable for pouncing.

James wished he had a gun since his Swiss army knife required close contact with a man who was expert at close contact kills. "I'm here to trade my life for my sister's."

Taken off guard by James' uncharacteristic assertiveness, Robespierre removed his thick glasses and tucked them in his Bohemian blouse, confirming James' suspicion that they were merely part of his disguise. "I didn't expect you to be so cooperative."

"This isn't cooperation, it's competition. I came to win back my sister."

"Why do you care about Seabright? She doesn't care about you," he laughed. Opening his black bag, he pushed the "play" button on his tape recorder which spewed a disjointed series of spiteful comments Seabright had made about her brave brother.

James could not hide his pain, but neither was he willing to share it with a man who thrived on venom. The floodlit gargoyle nearest him laughed at his predicament. The American stared at the glittering candlestick upriver where all his trouble started. It didn't seem possible that something as beautiful as the Eiffel Tower could be the scene of a senseless murder. "You spliced that tape. It's a bunch of lies," he growled, knowing some of it was probably true.

"The police don't seem to think so." Hawk stuck his wrists through the metal suicide netting as if it were his jail cell. "You're a wanted man. Seabright is a wanted woman. Neither of you is wanted by me, however."

James winced, knowing his sister was listening from inside the tower. "Speaking of the cops, how do you know they didn't hide up here until the tourists left the way you did?"

"You wouldn't be so stupid as to alert me to the fact they were hiding up here if they were hiding up here," Hawk laughed. "It requires premeditation to remain in the towers when you know the lights are going off. Few people pack flashlights. I see you didn't."

"The cops could be on the uppermost section of either tower where the bells bong."

"Do you really think I didn't check those chambers before swooping down for our little meet 'n' greet? *Il a le diable au corps!* I may be evil, but I'm not stupid," he howled.

"You're stupid enough to think your evil won't catch up with you. I know you just made this tape to hurt me because I hurt you on that champagne and chateaux tour, but I didn't mean to hurt you. I'm sorry. I'm sorry the victim hurt you, too. That's why you bonked him with the *boules* ball under the Eiffel Tower that night, right?"

"Wrong. I poisoned him. Smashing skulls is not subtle enough for the Eiffel's cameras, but the ball served its purpose since it implicated both of you, at least you thought it did." He spit over the edge. "I set you both up to take a fall, so either you go down or the naif does."

"Or you do." James skillfully positioned the priest so that Seabright could hear his awful admissions. "My suspicions were accurate indeed. Robespierre and Hawk are the same person." James held his breath when Seabright popped her head out to hear Robespierre's reply.

"My real name is Egbert Schmell from Omaha, but I am also the Hawk you hate. But you're no Honest Abe yourself. You pretended your name was James Woodlawn."

"My name is James Woodlawn, it's James Woodlawn Seabright."

Sensing something was wrong, Robespierre cocked his head to listen for a moment, then he spun on his boot heel and marched toward the spiraling staircase where Seabright and Parker were hiding. James knew there was nowhere for them to go except down the dark corridor of stone. Parker prompted Seabright to embark on the downward spiral, but she would have none of it. She stormed out of the tower, all piss and vinegar, to confront Robespierre. Parker remained hidden to maintain the element of surprise.

Since it was obvious Seabright had her heart set on throwing someone other than herself over the edge, James used his athletic prowess to restrain her. "I can't believe my ears!" she fulminated. Thinking a famous quotation would add just the right touch to her touché, she blurted out, "Euripides was right: 'The facts speak for themselves,' you scoundrel!"

"Facts are just the fictions we believe, and what you believe is your problem." He flexed the fingers on his gloves to make a point that he was wearing them for a pernicious purpose.

"You're a fraud, a fruitcake, and the Eiffel Tower killer! I can't believe it!"

"You can't believe it because you don't want to believe it."

She knocked the rest of the flowers off his headband. "You deliberately deceived me!"

"*Au contraire,* you deceived yourself. The reason that you love me is the reason that you leave me: you were asking for trouble, and you got what you asked for," Robespierre replied.

"To quote your hero, Hemingway, 'Bless me father, for you have sinned,'" she quipped, glad she wasn't too intimidated to quip. "What kind of father would frame an innocent student?"

"The father of lies? Don't feign innocence. You knew what I was when you met me."

"What you are is a loser, and you're going to lose big on Judgment Day. Someone ought to frame your fat face...with rope!"

"Fools like you are easy to frame," he laughed with vicious pleasure. "Backsliders are fun to blackmail. Their guilt holds them hostage, which makes it easy for me to hold them hostage, preferably in a tower such as this where tourists trample pearls like swine on their agnostic pilgrimages to the new Enlightenment. Isn't Notre Dame a perfectly lovely place to torture a confession out of someone on a vulgar Sunday afternoon?"

"You disgust me beyond words. I see that all the bristles in your broom mustache sprouted back overnight. Is that a dead caterpillar you glued on to your face?"

"I think it was still alive when I poked those pins into it." His belly giggled like jelly as he reached into his black bag.

James lunged for the valise then hurled it over the side of the tower. Hoping it landed safely in the Seine, he was sorry to see it had taken a sacrilegious detour onto a flying buttress.

"There goes my wool coat and wingtips," Robespierre laughed as if it all were just a game to him. "I rather enjoyed hearing you talk about the weirdo in the wool coat and wingtips, knowing said wool coat and wingtips were under my arm the whole time."

Hating all that she had enlisted to entice the perverted priest, she tugged on her hair as if it were a nest of serpents that had attached themselves to her brain. "When I passed out up on Montmartre, the man in a wool coat in wingtips who scooped me up was none other than you?"

"*Certainement.* I popped a little poison in your drink, hoping you would blab your brother's address to me, but there must be love underneath all that hurt, because you wouldn't divulge any family secrets." He held his hand over his heart mockingly. "You didn't pass out, either. I made that up. You only took a nipper's nap inside the crypt of Sacre Coeur."

Seabright leaned over the medieval ledge to see if she could spot the illuminated ice cream domes of Montmartre. "I didn't ride around the neon windmill of the Moulin Rouge, either?"

He snapped his fingers in her face, mortally wounding her pride. "Noooooo. I fabricated each of those episodes, so you'd feel as if you were out of control and in need of me, love."

"Don't call me love! I hate you! I hate me! I hate everything!"

"All that hate is just your love talking."

She looked for something to throw at him. "Shut up with your slippery semantics! Hell is gonna be mighty hot for heartless heretics like you! You don't even know what love is!"

"Neither do you. You think it's a week in the sheets with a priest who cheats."

James interjected since only the gargoyles were enjoying the unpleasantness. "Sis, you didn't love *him*, you loved *being in love* with him. Everything that is holy is healthy, and this guy is so unhealthy he makes me sick every time he opens his mouth. I think he put something in the wine he tried to get me to drink on the Seine cruise. The bottle was open when he gave it to me."

"Something with poison in it, I think, but attractive to the eye," Hawk taunted him.

"Another *Wizard of Oz* line. Your mannerisms were familiar, but your voice was so nasal on the cruise that it didn't click until Seabright told me you were an actor."

"A tissue tucked into an accommodating orifice did the trick."

"Your voice was weird, but I thought your glass-black eyes belonged to Hawk."

"But Robespierre's eyes aren't glass-black. Look at them," Seabright protested as if willing to purchase a quart of hope on the black market of make-believe.

"They're colored contacts," said Robespierre with a mocking cruelty.

"I hate you, but with any luck I will soon progress to a comfortable indifference."

James held a hand up in either direction to keep them from tearing each other limb from limb, something he was sure Hawk had some experience in doing to others. "Don't push your luck, sis. In case you weren't listening, he intends to kill me."

"I intend to kill both of you." Robespierre removed his broom mustache and ponytail hairpiece, then he ripped his eyebrow ring out of his skull to gross them out. Basking in their fear, he held the fake hair to his chin and stuck out his tongue like the gargoyle nearest him.

The athletic American wanted to use Hawk's skull as a shot-put. "I see that Paris's theater of lights has attracted some of the world's most unforgiving creatures: humans."

Too hot with anger to be afraid, Seabright let it rip: "Your heart isn't art; it's a deadly spider's web full of circular reasoning. How dare you call yourself a minister—you're a monster!"

"You wanted me to be a priest, so that's what I became. You thought I was married to God, yet you wanted me to cheat on my mate. Cheaters can't be choosers." Robespierre offered her his new skull ring in lieu of a wedding ring, but she fought back vomit when she realized he had removed it from his latest victim, probably with the finger still on it. "As is said in *Summa Theologica:* 'Beauty is a bitter, galling thing, as shocking as sin in the sanctuary, when it proves a mirage enticing the heart to the embrace of emptiness or evil,'" he laughed while snapping the fingers on his rubber gloves.

"How dare a disciple of the devil quote a saint like Thomas Aquinas?"

James rotated his head back and forth as if at Wimbledon to keep an eye on each of them. "Satan co-opts Scripture for his vile purposes. We learned that in Deception 101, remember?"

"I didn't sign up for that course."

"You signed up for my course instead." Robespierre swirled the blood on his eyebrow into Modern Art. "Good students play hooky when they see the devil at the blackboard."

She shook her hair like a rock star on the rocks. "You're the devil incarnate."

"I am that I am and that ain't Spam." He spit at the "Dei" word on James' jacket.

Little Red Riding Hood looked distractedly at the lights twinkling like diamonds across the European capital, diamonds that cut her heart instead of being cut to be mounted on her ring finger. "How can Paris be so pretty, and this turn out so ugly?"

"Sin has always been ugly," said James quietly but confidently, wiping the spit off "God." "I'm sorry you had to go through this to realize how truly ugly your pretty priest really is."

Robespierre held his flashlight under his face to accentuate his alleged ugliness. "My spirit guide told me I needed to connect with male energy to reach the next level of evolvement. That's when I went looking for a boy toy like the lad I poisoned under the Eiffel."

Seabright wanted to break a bottle over his head. "Why did you do this to me?"

"Because you let me." He fondled the jewelry draped against his hairy chest.

She paced back and forth across the stone balcony, wondering if the suicide netting were merely cosmetic or could stand up to the full force of her fury. Annoyed by the floodlights that blinded them from below, she barked at the sinister minister: "I should've known you were a wolf in sheep's clothing. Everything you said was a self-righteous reinterpretation of Scripture. You kept saying, 'Nothing is written, nothing is written,' but something is written, Robespierre with the big derriere: murderers, fornicators, and liars shall have their place in the lake of fire!"

"I didn't teach you anything that some liberal churches aren't teaching."

"Then you can put a pat of butter on them, too, because they're toast." Seabright's hands shook as if she were riding Parker's Milwaukee Rattler. Guttural laughter disgorged from deep inside her as if something resident in her flesh were now mocking her. Digging her shoes into the holes in the fencing, she climbed part way up the metal netting before looping one arm after the other through the wire to suspend herself like a cross. "To tell you the truth, this is a bigggggg relief. I really didn't want to go to hell anyway."

Robespierre turned his back to her, or perhaps to the cross she had become, then he ratcheted his neck in a half circle. "*Mademoiselle*, I assure you, there is no hell."

"Be sure and tell the devil that when you get there." Her eyes reached for the stars and the moon, but they remained as cold and as distant as her false friend. "This earth is as close as I will ever get to hell, but this earth is as close as you will ever get to heaven. Heretics are in for one helluva hangover when their party on earth is over."

"What makes you think you won't burn in the brimstone along with me?"

"I'm repenting, right here and right now." She closed her eyes and prayed defiantly. "I won't make two sorrows out of one. I'm cutting my losses, so I don't lose my soul."

His eyes mocked her. "Little Red Riding Hood has come a lonnnng way in her thinking."

"Yeah, full circle!" Her face hardened with every word even though her body hung as limp as a rag doll. "I ought to expose you. Maybe I'll write a book about you. A satire."

"Authors need to be alive to pursue their craft." Robespierre scribbled something in thin air with his bloody finger while smiling at them to give them the finger. "Maybe I could get that pen from the morgue for you, the one you loaned me at the Eiffel that will implicate you."

"You are as two-faced as a Roman coin. I'll never ever trust a man of the cloth again."

"I prefer to think of myself as a woman, actually." A cop appeared in the square below and seemed to be looking up at them. "I guess this is where I make my exit, stage left."

"Aren't you going to kill us first?" Seabright taunted him with ill-timed snottiness.

"Change of plans. I do it my way, or I come back another day."

"You can't do squat without your kill bag, can you," she sneered, drunk with rage.

"I prefer the element of surprise. I'll be throwing you that surprise party soon."

"But you bragged that you were going to kill us," she egged him on, hoping someone would end her life so she wouldn't have to face her folly for the rest of her life.

"It's a 'woman's' prerogative to change his mind," James interrupted them, his eyes locked like lasers on the homely heretic, self-assured in his own stupidity.

He tugged on his wrist stitches with his teeth. "Click your heels three times and this nocturnal panorama of Paris will be the last view of earth your eyes will ever look upon."

She leapt off the netting and landed squarely in his face. "Putting you in charge of a church is as dangerous as putting the real Robespierre in charge of The Committee of Public Safety. I should kill you with my bare hands for the sake of the public's safety!"

"Careful," said James, worried she might do the unthinkable without giving it a second thought. "You are reeling in a roiling sea of rejection, and those are shock-infested waters."

She shook her head as if auditioning for *The Exorcist,* whiplash notwithstanding. "I must take my leave of you, mates." Robespierre highstepped to the tower entrance like a Lippinzaner in leotards then spun around to flip them off. "*A bientot! Au revoir!*"

James looked at Seabright. Seabright looked at James. Neither thought it entirely sane to attempt to apprehend a serial killer on a ledge overlooking Paris at night, so they watched in horror as he disappeared down the dark, spiraling staircase.

"Parker is on those stairs!" James gasped. The athlete dashed into the staircase entrance but was forced to stop a few steps from the top. The path of flickering light from the killer's flashlight disappeared down the dark hole with his fading footsteps. James braced himself for an audible confirmation of Robespierre's unpleasant introduction to Parker. Not hearing anything climactic, James fumbled his way to fresh air, panicked about the possibilities that presented themselves. "I couldn't follow him without a flashlight," he explained.

Seabright snapped out of her self-induced tailspin after seeing the handwriting on the wall. "We have to help Parker! Hawk could be trying to kill him even as we speak!"

"Hawk?"

"Yes! Robespierre was a figment of my sin-soaked imagination!"

"And his." James rushed to the ledge and looked down. "There he goes! He's leaving the tower! Stop that man in the pantyhose and pantaloons!" he yelled to the tourists below.

Hawk disappeared into the crowd as nonchalantly as a choirboy. James' crisscrossed the square with his eyes again, hoping to find Parker had somehow descended the stairs safely before the killer ran down them. Then a flame drew his eye to the left. "Who's there?" he asked the gargoyle that looked as if it were lighting up to smoke.

"One mortified motorcycle missionary at your service," Parker announced while waving the souvenir cigarette lighter he bought just for the occasion.

"You changed hiding places," James gasped with a sigh of relief as his uncle stepped out of the niche that led up to the last leg of the tower.

"Why didn't you stop Hawk?" Seabright asked.

"I was in no position to stop anyone. I waited for a good opportunity, but opportunity never knocked. I was hoping he would turn his back to me just once so I could jump him, but after you two engaged in your verbal volleyball, he headed straight for me. Had he not turned around to flip you off, you might have found me at the bottom of the stairs with a flashlight embedded in my face and pantyhose over my mouth. That outburst bought me my freedom."

"That's when you made a run for it?"

"Yup. I skedaddled on all fours to the tippy-top where not even the gargoyles trust the footing, but I'm no action hero. I almost plunged to the ground while looking for another way down from the tower. I thought Hawk was coming after me, but I guess he went down, instead."

"Down, down, down like a balloon blown through with buckshot," she sighed.

"A lot of good this rendezvous did," James griped as he stared at the tourists milling below. "The cops should've stopped him. I can't believe he got away with murder."

"He might murder again," Parker speculated while praying for potential victims.

"It's us he wants to murder," Seabright admitted, her face as sunken as the Titanic.

Parker gave her shoulder a hug. "First, we have to hope that someone down there turns the lights on up here, so we can see our way down these tortuous steps."

"But if someone turns the staircase lights on and comes up here, we'll have to explain what we're doing up here, which will probably occasion an untimely arrest," she lamented.

"Two of us could be booked for murder just as Hawk planned," James added.

"He said he's coming back for us another day," Seabright added pensively.

"Then let's form a human chain and tiptoe down the spiraling stairs using my souvenir cigarette lighter," Parker decided for them.

A tear shot out of her eye and blew up on the cold balcony, but no longer was she entertaining the notion of throwing herself off it. "Why did I let myself go out on a limb like that for a hellbound heretic?"

"Were you happy while you were out on that limb?" Parker sympathized.

"Happy out of my mind."

"Then that's why you did it, and never mind the rest right now. Been there, done that. Been *here* and done that, as a matter of fact. Twain said, 'I reckon we are all fools.'"

James squeezed her elbow tenderly. "Did you read *The Imitation of Christ* while you were at Civitas Dei? Thomas a Kempis admitted, 'I am taught by my own hurt.'"

"That's an understatement. My knees will never be the same when I'm done repenting of this fiasco." She couldn't believe she was going to hold the hands of the two people she had hoped would disappear from the French landscape. "That creep can't get away with this!"

"Nobody gets away with anything," Parker reassured her. "*Nobody.*"

CHAPTER TWENTY

Bernkastel, Germany
7:07 p.m. 7 March

Deep in the heart of the Mosel valley, in a German river village called Bernkastel decorated postcard-cute with half-timbered houses and cobble lanes, a lone cruise boat puttered under the Bahnhofstrasse Bridge which linked the *Spitzhauschen* to a Renaissance *Rathaus*, Medieval marketplace, Saint Michael's fountain, *Graacher Tor* gate and a pedestrian path which the pedestrians desperately needed to find the *Spitzhauschen,* Renaissance *Rathaus*, Medieval marketplace, Saint Michael's fountain and the *Graacher Tor* gate.

Jutting out over the narrow lanes like white cardboard boxes, immaculate inns outlined with big brown beams overlapped the quaint shops below that advertised their wares with old fashioned symbols on iron signs. Born with picturesque charm, Bernkastel felt sleepy and safe to Parker in the off season before the spring floods arrived, floods of tourists. He paused to look up at the hilltop castle, now bathed in a golden light, which he and his niece had ridden to on rented scooters during daylight hours while James practiced shot-putting melons on the riverbank.

"I can't believe a week has flown by since we fled Paris." Danielle Seabright snarfed down a pile of German *Petersilienkartoffein* the size of Texas that were gushing with just as much oil. "Finding out about Ropespierre was a rude awakening, but it put the brakes on my backsliding. I've come back to the country of everlasting clarity, to quote Kempis. That *Buchhandlung* Bible I bought down by the riverbank fudge shop is now my *Kilometre Zero.*"

"*Ja oui!*" Parker cheered. "The B.I.B.L.E. is Basic Instructions Before Leaving Earth."

James rubbed his aching biceps. "Sin has such a short memory. The Israelites proved that with their intermittent idolatry. As soon as I indulge in sin I remember instantly what's wrong with it, but too often I don't remember those lessons I'm sure I'll never forget." He glanced at the wad of *Deutsche Marks* stacked like napkins on top of the old wooden table. "You did return that wallet you found at the *Schreibwarengeschaft,* didn't you, Danielle?"

"You bet. They use euros now, so this is a souvenir stash of cash. I also made restitution for my filching that *fromage* in France. It feels good to hear you call me Danielle again so that I don't think I can commit secret sins using a bogus name. I'm going to be radically obedient, because I now know *all* good things come from God's garden of delights. I chased forbidden fruit, and he wound up being a fruitcake!" she laughed out loud.

"The *Tierarzt* was so surprised to have his wallet returned, and apparently so wealthy, that he gave your sister a reward," Parker added. "She has enough euros to buy a used enduro."

"That's what I'll need to criss-cross the cobblestone quarters of Paris. I've been studying the maps so I'll be ready to rip around Montmartre as a motorcycle missionary when I return."

"Get one with training wheels," James teased, "so I can make a victory lap around the Eiffel Tower if I win Worlds after my regime of shot-putting melons by the Mosel."

"Speaking of the Eiffel Tower, is there any news about Hawk yet? I don't give a rip about him, but neither do I want him ripping us to pieces when we return to Paris."

"No news isn't good news in this case, but God will eventually throw a rope around Robespierre, hammer Hawk, and ensnare Egbert, assuming he hasn't assumed another identity already. However, we can't hide here forever," Parker replied while leafing through his sermon notes from a village *Kirche* called Bad Munster where the munster was anything but bad.

"The cops know everything we know. Thank God they believed us," said Danielle.

"Three witnesses singing the same song didn't hurt," James chimed in.

Parker stared at a wrought iron sign that dangled over the winding medieval lane like a Sword of Damocles. In the cellar below the sign he had met secretly with his mistress once upon a time, a woman who thought she could do no wrong if she slept all right.

"The owner brought us another plate of free *Kase*. This prodigal is being thrown a party."

James puffed out both his cheeks. "You sure can eat since you quit drinking."

"I forgot how good food tastes. It's better than grog and doesn't make you groggy."

Parker pinned a Deutschland pin on his hat. "*Jeder Tag ist ein kleines Leben,* every day is a little life. I filled a shopping cart with natural pleasures when I quit drinking."

"Natural pleasures?"

"Greek salad, fudge, java, water skis, biker stuff, travel guides to exotic ports of call, memorable movies—fun stuff that isn't forbidden. Focusing on all the good stuff God put in the Garden makes the poison apples seem less appealing. I call it 'replacement theology' because I replace something I know I shouldn't have with something I know I should. Otherwise, the void created from quitting certain sins forms a vacuum that can suck you right back into them."

"*Tres* true. When I think about the one thing I can't have, it's all I want."

"Pal around with people who don't dabble. France is the cheese capital of the planet, and many shops have their own cheese cellars, so delight yourself in the cheese instead of the wine. This barrister doesn't mind admitting Paris has three times as many chefs as lawyers."

James flexed a smoked-cheese *Schichtkase* as if it were a barbell. "Oceanographers have yet to document the fact, but there are riptides in rum, tidal waves in tequila, and waterspouts in wine. I wish more pastors would spell out the spiritual dangers of drinking."

"Then they'd have to stop drinking themselves," Parker chuckled. "Some are closet drinkers, and nobody is going to come out of the closet if the leaders stay in there. I've grown fond of the Scripture that says, 'I am sober for your cause.' There isn't time for sloppy *agape.*"

The athlete on the run added his two cents. "I think our ears affect our emotions more than anything else. Tunes can take you to places you don't want to go faster than any fluid."

"Nudie numnums are my nemesis." The legal eagle held up his menu as if it were a centerfold. "If you ever see my nose in a skin magazine that isn't *Zits Digest*, spank me."

"A doctor said alcohol tries to destroy every organ in your body—your brain, heart, eyes, skin, liver, muscles, kidneys and sex organs. *Ipso facto,* it's poison. I think there must be spirits in spirits. I doubt I would've listened to Hawk had I not been drinking. Maybe he knew it."

"Of course he knew it," said James. "Alcohol is your Achilles heel, and Satan targets our wounds and weaknesses. Some friend—he pretends to come to the rescue just to finish us off."

Parker thumbed his suspenders. "Faust became hellbent on rewriting the Bible *after* he sold his soul to the devil. He brayed: 'It seems absurd. I must translate it otherwise.' That describes Robespierre's rebellious revisionism to a tee. His allegiance is to the Abyss."

Danielle pointed at two bears that were climbing brazenly into a fountain outside. She soon realized the bears were brazen in more ways than one; they were also made of brass.

"Germany is more colorful than France, but the air is too redolent with wine for my feet to enjoy safe footing here. A tourist booklet owns up to the intended enticement, advertising the many intoxications expected to follow the fragrance emanating from the wine cellars." Parker pointed at a portrait of three generations of drunkards and diapered drunkards-to-be.

Little Red Riding Hood applied her silverware to the table to simulate a drumroll. "I made up my own temptation termination quote: Rebellion foments where grapes ferment."

"*Ja oui,*" Parker agreed. "But Bernkastel also has some evocative aids to devotion to keep one's eyes focused on eternity. There's a melodramatic crucifix at the end of Mandatstrasse street, and the mourners are actually chiseled right into the base of the cross."

"It also helps to substitute the sin we don't see in ourselves for the sin we see so clearly in others. Gluttony is as bad as sexual sin; sexual sin is as bad as self-pity; self-pity is as bad as bad music; bad music is as bad as spiritual pride, speeding, swearing, lying, sloth, envy etcetera. The devil's menu reads 'No Substitutions,' so we'll focus on others' faults and never see our own."

"The devil took advantage of you when you let your guard down and stuck your nose up, but he didn't do anything to you that he doesn't do to anyone who lets him."

Danielle's face soured like a German potato salad. "What a 'coincidence.' When I asked Robespierre why he was doing this to me, he replied, 'Because you let me.' I think I'll refer to this episode in my life as 'The Paris Plot' to remind myself of Satan's plot to ruin my life."

"If we dine in the devil's kitchen, we're what's in the oven," said James with a dollop of shame as he shook a bottled brown goop that Germans called ketchup for some reason.

Parker lobbed a potato ball at him. "We're in Luther Land, so here's an apropos aphorism: 'The Bible is alive, it speaks to me; it has feet, it runs after me; it has hands, it lays hold on me.' Genesis 50:20 assures us: 'What Satan intended for evil, God can use for good.'"

Danielle felt like cutting her hair since the memory of tossing it about coquettishly brought waves of shame. "Deception is a drug. I actually thought I was becoming more loving when I started hating Christians. Isaiah 5:20 is *tres* true. Robespierre said you were inhibiting my cosmic evolvement. He's a big *bete noire* in my book All the nails are in his coffin."

Preoccupied with some emotional horror of his own, Parker twisted the chain on his biker wallet around and around his finger until it cut off the circulation. Danielle undid the chain, realizing it was her turn to take care of him. "Are you all right?"

Parker screwed his leather cap back and forth across his forehead as if trying to kill a hangover. "It hurts to be here. Memories of my sin swamp my soul like a septic tsunami. Being bad up at the castle was fun while it lasted, but the remorse has lasted a lifetime."

James bounced a *Zahnstocher* off his forehead. "Don't let your mind take your heart to places where your body shouldn't go. Memories can be deadly detours."

Danielle chimed in, "You said you hated yourself and everyone else when it ended."

"Hate is just a heart with an arrow in it. I loved her even when I hated her. You don't hate people you never loved. Hurt naturally transmogrifies into hate. Dining on Rhine wine made it easy to do things we'd always regret. It seemed as if we were always laughing, but when we looked into a mirror, we saw two people crying. We had left the Garden."

"The only thing you had in common was that you were miserable when you were apart. That fling is so far in the past that you no longer see it for what it was, only for what it was not."

"It was not a lot of things, including not right," Parker voiced his compunction. "I made a career out of learning things the hard way, but God has blessed me with double for my trouble."

"I never heard the whole story." James made it sound like a question. "I knew you used to be a minister, but how did a minister manage to get involved with another woman?"

"The same way anyone else does. I rationalized one thing after another until I was light years from the Light. I hated the Light, that's why I print John 3:19 on my t-shirts instead of just John 3:16. More ministers fall than midwives since the pride of their position makes the pulpit a very slippery place. I love the half-timbered architecture that surrounds us, because it's a visual metaphor of the man I want to become—as clean and solid on the outside as I am on the inside."

"Do you think Robespierre was really a reverend once upon a time?" Danielle asked.

"Maybe. Fruit can go bad. You'd think God would extinguish such flaming heretics, but II Thessalonians 2:10-12 suggests God lets some false teachers serve as magnets to attract those who want to be deceived into one place, so they don't infect every congregation on the planet."

She tapped his *Kaffee* mug with an infamous Civitas Dei pen. "These new apostate anonymous cards you designed have turned the Land of Lederhosen into a hospital for my heart."

"Really?" His boyish grin returned, erasing the fissure of his frown.

"*Ja oui.*" She kissed him on the cheek. "Thanks for taking care of me."

"Taking care of you takes care of me."

"I owe a great debt to you. Had it not been for you, I might've done a swan dive off the Eiffel Tower when I was ambushed by my sin. That just goes to show you that everything about the devil is down. Don't let your spiritual lapses here in Germany get you down, Parker."

The Bible biker covered his eyes with his hand, capitulating without words.

"'The person who makes no mistakes makes nothing at all,'" Danielle read to Parker from his own card. "'I will make up to you the years the swarming locust has eaten.' Joel 2:25. You lawyers are Latin lovers, so you'll like this quote you found for me. *Virescit vulnere virtus*. Virtue flourishes from a wound. I think vicarious virtue flows from Christ's wounds to ours."

"That's why Talbot sings about Jesus' heart being an open wound of love. I like this French phrase from Jacques Maritain: 'God educates us through our deceptions and mistakes.'"

James high-fived his sister as she showed him the new apostates anonymous card. "You put some Deuteronomy on these cards? I love Deuteronomy. It's kick-butt black-and-white."

"Robespierre hated all things black-and-white, especially the Bible," Danielle added.

"People enamored with gray love their own gray matter. Deuteronomy 30 reads, 'You shall return and obey the voice of the Lord...then the Lord your God will make you most prosperous in all the work of your hands, for the Lord will again delight in prospering you.'"

It dawned on Danielle that the yellow blobs on her plate were supposed to be scrambled eggs, though *Hoppel-Poppel* sounded like a less gooey life form. "I hear hope in Romans 8:28. 'We know God causes all things to work together for good to those who love God.'"

"God probably works all things for bad for rebels who hate God," said the biker-barrister. The expatriate stared longingly out the window, hoping there was another half-timbered treasure like Bernkastel that would serve as a vacation from his pain instead of a voyage back into it. "I'm surprised Robespierre even believes in the resurrection."

"He believes in the resurrection of our repressed sexuality, not the resurrection of Christ, except on a metaphysical level, whatever that means. His definitions change with his desires."

"Bohn said, 'The Devil entangles youth with beauty...and the learned with false doctrine.' False teaching is fatal, so I put Isaiah 29:24 on my new apostates anonymous cards: 'They that erred in spirit shall come to understanding, and they that murmured shall learn doctrine.'"

"Here are more marvelous maxims: 'Even from the stump of a fallen tree, new growth can emerge. It's never too late to become what you should have been.' James can still make the Olympics, and I can still pen a novel about deception." Danielle glanced at the mini Impressionist painting of Notre Dame on her new vitamin box. "I'll never forget the fun I had with him up on Montmartre, what I remember of it." Her face creased with frowns of frustration as she reminisced despite the danger. "Maybe French fathers are just different..."

"He isn't French! He isn't a father! Snap out of it!" Parker waved his felt hat in front of her eyes. "C.S. Lewis said, 'To be greatly and effectively wicked a man needs some virtue.' Proverbs 12:10 similarly warns, 'The tender mercies of the wicked are cruel.'"

"He was so gentle, so generous, so willing to be misunderstood..."

"You couldn't understand him because he changed his theology more often than his undies! He made up his religion based on his own opinions. Like the Ten Commandments, Luke 17:32 is a sermon in stone: Remember Lot's wife! Start looking back, and you might turn back!"

•

James made a megaphone out of his Mosel Valley placemat then announced: "Need I remind you that we don't know where Hawk-Robespierre-Egbert is right now?"

"I bet he's not in Omaha, but I bet his first *corpus delicti* is there," said Parker.

Danielle's reveries disappeared like dandelions in the wind. "*Gut gutachten!* He could be stepping off the Trier-Koblenz train at this very moment, hiding in one of these narrow alleys between the fudge shops, or camping out in the castle high above the village. He's playing chess with us, but he's going to hear 'Checkmate!' when God is done playing chess with him."

"Speaking of games, I have to return to Paris tomorrow, or I'll miss World Competition. I can't keep competing in my mind and expect to win with my body," said James.

"Actually, there is some news. Hawk vacated his apartment and disappeared into thin air." Parker flexed a *Windbeutel* roll, sending its cream center into orbit like a sugary afterburner. "We probably won't have the satisfaction of seeing a quick resolution to this conflict."

James watched another cream puff explode. "Vengeance is mine, saith the Lord."

"One thing I've learned ugly but learned well is that God takes His time. I would rather have that rat show up at the train station today, so we could have the blessed assurance that he won't show up in our sleep, but it's not our job to go after him."

The strapping winner-wannabe draped his arm around Danielle. "Would you consider flying home from Frankfurt instead of endangering your derriere with a risky return to Paris?"

"Not a chance! I plan to kick Satan's butt by redeeming the territory I turned over to that spiritual con. Each place where I backslid, I'm going to slide back into God's win column."

"I noticed you've been tucking tracts in every wine rack we wander by, and I saw Parker stick an entire Bible in the *Trockenbeerenauslese* wine cellar where he got soused with his sassy lass, but Bernkastel ain't Paris, sis. I'm not comfortable with your returning to Paris."

"I'm not comfortable with any of us returning to Paris, but we're all on track and not looking back, so what's the worse that could happen? If we die, we go to heaven. I'm dying to write about deception, and what better place to write about it than where it happened? Every view will be a visual *aide-memoire*. I'll pen my penance. Like Samson, I'll use my mistake to God's advantage, sending Hawk's temple of intellectual idolatry collapsing in on him."

"But it collapsed on Samson, too. Remember?"

"I'll try not to let that happen." She bought a mini java to go. "Parker, do you know of some pavement café by Notre Dame where I can camp out and create for free?"

"The only pavement café that's free is that pavement that is a café. It costs about 7 bucks for a jolt of java at a joint along the Seine, *sans* refills. But you can huddle between the *bouquinistas* and absorb more ambience than can be put into words."

"I'm also going to find some way to help the forgotten in our midst like the elderly."

"You won't find them in the pricey places where you plan to park butt," said James.

"Try a *maison* for the aged or some cemetery other than the one where Robespierre hung out in," Parker suggested. "Cemeteries are perfect for perfecting your riding skills, too."

"That sounds like a plan. I'll write in the morning and visit deadland in the afternoon." She shut her eyes tight as if praying. "I can see an old woman cold with pain. She's hobbling across the uneven lanes, looking for someone to help her. Maybe that someone is me..."

CHAPTER TWENTY-ONE

Montmartre, Paris
6 p.m. 9 March

Parker waved his Parisian newspaper at Danielle as she sipped a *café creme* on his balcony, her Bible in her lap. "A man matching Robespierre's description was just arrested on the French Riviera. There was a garbled message on my answering machine that referred to Nice, but I thought he was referring to my nice niece, you. I'll call the cop shop to verify the story. I guess it was safe for us to return to Paris after all."

Danielle crossed herself, a custom she planned to continue no matter which country she called home. "My blood runs cold to think I daydreamed of rendezvousing with Robespierre in the Riviera. Hawk the heretic probably has himself a hide out down there. My face could have wound up floating face down in front of the cameras of the Cannes film festival."

"I hope no one else floats before his time." Parker followed the story to a back page of the paper that pictured a Parisian "motorcycle" outfitted for winter with detachable mitts, mud flaps, and a wraparound rubber windshield that looked as if it had done time as a dumpster liner before being inducted into the biker world. "Yup, they nabbed Hawk outside Casino Noir."

"God knew we were too emotionally involved to execute His will without executing Hawk in the process. I'm now focused on my Savior, not *savoir faire.* I hope Hawk knows it."

"I knows it," he teased as he read the Scripture stickers on her new helmet. "This world is just a bridge to the next, and it doesn't make sense to build your home on a bridge. I'm here to help people pack their suitcases for eternity elsewhere, their final home away from home."

"I'm afraid an old hunchbacked woman I've been watching down in coffinville is about to head home. Parker, It's just the sort of scenario you suggested in Germany."

"I suggested a home for the aged or some cemetery *other* than this one."

"Like you said, those traffic-free lanes are perfect for practicing my biking skills, and Hawk is behind bars now. I know the Lord is already working in that lady's life."

"How do you know that?" he asked, trying not to deposit any doubt in her heart.

"I've been praying for her, that's how, and I know God hears my prayers now. Nothing makes you bolder than a clear conscience, and nothing cripples you faster than a guilty one."

"Unconfessed sin eviscerates evangelism. You don't dare preach at someone if you haven't preached to yourself. How do you think Hawk is surviving his guilty conscience?"

"Like most people, he probably seared his conscience years ago. I Timothy 4 and Ephesians 4 describe the reprobate result of rejecting God. Robespierre *is* Romans 1. But I've been praying that God will reactivate the nerves of his seared conscience so he'll repent."

"If he were to suddenly feel the impact of his sin, he'd probably kill himself."

"Better himself than somebody else."

She savored an exotic juice with her java, knowing they were nourishing her body back to health. "Do you think his constant consumption of cocktails cooked his conscience?"

"Was Napolean a narcissist? Is Louis the XIV furniture? Drinking inflamed a fire that was already raging inside him, but the body will eventually reject the man who rejects God."

"I still feel pretty rejected myself, but I'm not looking back, so I'll stay on track."

"That's another good verse for a hearse. Don't waste your pain. Pain can be a fruit factory if you let the Holy Spirit produce pure pineapples of peace, mangos of meekness, lemons of love, papayas of patience, and figs of faith. I get good mileage out of my mistakes."

"The Left Bank is captivating in the early morning light, but I can only write for so long before I start doodling gargoyles. That's why I came back to see if that hunchback is in the cemetery again, and if not her, then some other soul like her whose toes are teetering on eternity."

Parker handed her the binoculars. "I'll go with you when my last client leaves."

"I haven't seen her come around at night. Maybe she ran into Robespierre once upon a time and thought twice about moonlight strolls through the mortuary. He's in jail, so I need to put some more practice miles on my motorcycle. If I loop around its lanes two thousand times tomorrow, maybe I won't crash into a chestnut cart when I wheel up to Place du Tertre."

"If I'm running late, will you take James with you? After a week in Bernkastel, my clients are racked 'n' stacked something awful. I know you're revved to redeem the time as an enduro evangelist, but that cemetery is a place where you and you-know-who used to hang out, and I don't want the memories to wipe you off your feet like an apostate avalanche."

"James is competing now, and he has no wheels." She tried to find the Eiffel Tower with his spy glasses, knowing it would impact her differently after coming clean. "I feel drawn to return to that cemetery to reclaim the turf of my turpitude, so get home as soon as you can."

"Memories can transmogrify themselves into deadly seductions," Parker warned.

"I really don't see that happening. In spiritual warfare, the best defense is a good offense. Besides, what's the worse that could happen? I repented, so if I die, I go to heaven. If the babushka grandma dies, she could go to hell. Redeeming souls is now my *raison d'etre.*"

"Death doesn't give you the chills like it did a week ago?" Parker chuckled.

"No. Looking at this sea of coffins feels like a sea of tranquility. I'm designing my own set of temptation termination cards, one of which includes a German sign I read at Bernkastel's Brotchen Bakery: The best reason to do the right thing today is *tomorrow*."

He toasted her with a mug of dark chocolate java laced with mint *glace*. "Memorize the goner's grocery list, I Corinthians 6:9,10. 'Do not be deceived: neither fornicators, nor idolaters, nor adulterers, nor homosexuals, nor thieves, nor covetous, nor drunkards...shall inherit the kingdom of God.' How many paper missionaries did you give safe passage to Montmartre?"

"A saddlebag's worth, not that my bike has saddlebags. Tying grapefruit netting to the frame doesn't exactly cut it, either. I need a job, but I need to take a French class first."

"Don't take the French class that James took. That's where he met Robespierre."

"Don't worry. I'm not going near Hawk's turf. I'll buy a phrase book instead."

A hearse cruised the graveyard below, but its disembodied passenger had already been delivered to a different address under the cemetery. "Make sure you strap on your metal skull cap when you crisscross the cobblestones. The devil wants to stop what you're doing."

"I'm going to make the devil pay for chasing my ambulance. I'll visit the grieving and aged until some old goat starts bleating and baa-ing in a wool coat, *sans* wingtips."

CHAPTER TWENTY-TWO

Montmartre Cemetery, Paris
Sunset 10 March

Danielle waited until dusk for Parker to return from his law office, but when she spotted the hunchback babushka grandma in the cemetery again, she decided to wait no longer. Mounting her enduro, she did a fun figure eight around the graveyard's winding lanes until the undulating terrain delivered her to the old woman's doorstep. The young American parked her two-wheeled transportation behind a sloped retaining wall so as not to scare the woman, then she tiptoed toward the bench where she once partied as if death were not on her doorstop.

Like concrete kennels restraining creatures from another world, Montmartre's monstrous mausoleums made the finality of death seem like a very big deal. The elderly woman with a face like a November pumpkin preoccupied herself with a calico cat that had gotten itself caught inside the picnic basket that Robespierre left for just such a grieving soul to find. Once the kitten had freed itself, it licked the widow's hands like lollipops, even though her hands were as worn as the leather on old baseball gloves. Montmartre's gargantuan stone crypts dwarfed the hobbled visitor like haughty bank vaults that had no time for a penniless client who carried plastic flowers instead of plastic money. Her steel wool hairdo and fake fur could not hide her poverty.

Danielle watched and waited, hoping not to startle the crippled mourner who blew her nose like a foghorn, apparently unaware of her presence. The granny scratched her chin, then she gave her butt a good scratch, as well. When she finally picked up her tattered purse and the discarded picnic basket to resume her somber stroll, Little

Red Riding Hood slipped between the tombstones and tapped her gently on the shoulder. "*Bonjour*? Hello? Grandmother?"

"No, the Big Bad Wolf!"

Danielle leapt on top of a granite coffin, her red cape catching on a decorative iron spear as she did so. Instinctively, she engaged in a deep breathing Lamaze exercise, absent the stirrups, fainting father, and pumpkin-sized product. "Robespierre? I thought you were in the Riviera!"

"You thought wrong." The hobbling hag stood up straight, dislodging his "hunchback."

"Who did they arrest in the Riviera matching your description?"

"Which description? Hawk the businessman? Eaton the English tart? Robespierre the revolutionary? Egbert Schmell the mortician? The Marais man I paid handsomely to imitate handsome me was none other than Jacques Monet, a con for all occasions."

She felt like clubbing him over the head with the Bible she brought to give the grieving grandmother. Hoping Parker had finally returned to his apartment, she waved her Bible to get him to look through his binoculars. "This book will conquer every con on the planet," she added to make the waving of her Bible look less like a signal.

"If you believed the Bible, you wouldn't act the way you do."

"The way I *did,* and your slick chicanery was a cold accomplice. Tolstoy also succumbed to sin for a season and wrote: 'Don't judge God's holy ideals by my inability to meet them.'"

Angry that she wasn't terrified of him, Robespierre tore open the pillow and made a storm of its feathers. "Parker will have an accident in five minutes, six if he circled the Etoile."

She bared her teeth to demonstrate her righteous resolve as she yanked his kerchief off his head. "What big fangs you have, grandmother. What did you do to Parker?"

He flipped her over his shoulder and into his lap, laughing like a drunken sailor. "Your interest in motorcycles sparked an interest in me, so I studied Parker's panhead so I'd know how to sabotage it, my pretty." He held his hands up behind his head like Big Bad Wolf ears.

"It's me you want, not him. He's done nothing to you."

"He made you suspect me."

"Yeah, because you're guilty!" she panted. "What is it you want from me?"

"Your soul. I bugged your room in Bernkastel with the bug the blue boys used on me. Irony does attend the best dramas, does it not? That's how I knew you would be looking for an old woman. I've dressed up in three different outfits in three different cemeteries, but I did not think you would be so stupid as to return to our happy hunting ground."

She punched and kicked at him as her eyes searched for the cemetery crew she was counting on to bail her out if her plan went bust. "Tell me what you did to Parker!"

"That would spoil the fun." He primped his wig like an aging actress who thought it was everyone else who was aging. "Dumpster diving can be *tres* enlightening, *mademoiselle*. Do you recognize this A-4 toll stub, or this menu map of the Mosel, or this Bernkastel brochure?" He held up each in turn. "I noticed you were a sucker for the silver heads that lounged about the Louvre, so I made myself into an old woman with a hint of homelessness. I figured you'd pay grandma a visit if you knew Robespierre was in jail in the south of France."

Danielle slumped to her knees to intercede unabashedly for her uncle.

"It's too late," he laughed. "I unscrewed the nut on his front fork so the wheel will shake loose on his Milwaukee Rattler. He probably bit pavement halfway up the Champs Elysees. One day you'll run over his remains with your own bike. I also severed the chin strap on his brain bucket below the earpiece, so if there is anything left of him, you'll be able to can it."

She wanted to scream, then she remembered the Scripture James taught her in Bernkastel: *Do not for a moment be intimidated by your adversaries, for such fearlessness will be a clear sign to them of their impending destruction. Philippians 1:28.*

"I'm killing two birds with one stone," he continued with uncharacteristic impatience as if his timing had been thrown off by something. "I don't fancy loose ends."

"Loose canons always leave loose ends." She knew she wasn't supposed to beat people over the head with the Bible, but she thought the occasion warranted it.

"You and Tame James will be booked as co-conspirators. What was your motive for killing your uncle, you ask? You wanted his Montmartre apartment, of course. Oh, and thanks for providing me with an entire week to create a paper trail that will implicate the both of you."

Tears welled up in her eyes as she realized what her sin was going to do to someone who had risked his life for her at a time when she was not willing to risk anything for him. She cocked her head sideways to hear better as a loud vehicle motored up the long lane that bisected the cemetery. Unfortunately, Robespierre also heard it. The stone retaining wall blocked her view, but she hoped the cemetery crew was finally returning.

Much to her chagrin, the motor stopped one lane short of the grave where Robespierre had taken cover. Not knowing what to do, Danielle couldn't believe her ears when a second vehicle circled the perimeter wall, a vehicle that sounded like a semi. Realizing the fake father, dressed like a mother, couldn't help but hear it, too, she leapt on to the bench to wave the vehicle down. The only wheels in sight, however, were the two wheels of a distant crotch rocket that looked as if it were being driven by a doper who didn't realize he was on it.

Her arms and legs pumping like oil derricks, Danielle bolted toward the circular path that looped under the blue bridge. She figured if the person on the rice rocket didn't stop to help her, a scream in the right direction might rouse the attention of the cemetery crew, although she knew said scream might also startle the caretakers who weren't used to seeing faces that didn't have daisies poking through their dentures.

As the speed bike zipped around the Old World lamposts, the American's young lips tried to form a French phrase that would motivate the oncoming motorcyclist to help her. It was then that she realized the big scooter was no rice burner but rather a yellow bike that looked an awful lot like Parker's panhead. As a matter of fact, it *was* Parker's panhead. Parker careened to a stop, then he flung his helmet like a dirty diaper as he raced across the pebbly landscape to rescue Danielle. "Are you ok? I came the minute I got your message, hon!"

She hugged him like a Teddy Bear in chaps. "What message?"

"The e-mail that said you had been kidnaped in the cemetery."

"I didn't send you any e-mail."

"I did." Robespierre shuffled toward them, his kill bag draped over his arm like a quiver.

Parker's eyes grew wide with disbelief. "It never crossed my mind that you didn't send it, Danielle. He even signed it with your new nickname, the enduro evangelist. The message warned me not to call the cops, or he would suffocate you with your own cape."

"There's no way you could tell it was Hawk on a computer screen," she consoled him.

"Don't you want to know how I got your e-mail address?" bragged the grandmotherly killer as he played a hopeless game of hopscotch on the headstones.

"Dumpster diving, I presume?"

"No, you logged into a Bible biker website at Kaffeezimmer Internet Café in Bernkastel and had a cyber chat with a teacher in the Aqua Algarve of Portugal. You were searching for a Christian for your nice niece to stay with since Paris didn't pan out for her."

"That was you?"

"*Certainement!* The Big Bad Wolf surfed the web looking for Little Red Riding Hood but found protective Parker instead. You motorcycle missionaries shouldn't have bothered crossing the Big Pond since your hogs don't float on the liberal lily pads of Europe."

"I plan to cross every pond, and double-cross pond scum like you."

Danielle tugged on Parker's *lederhosen,* whispering, "Did you call the cops or not?"

Robespierre snapped the straps on his granny garter. "There's no need for that. I came here to confess. The cops should be here within half an hour, half a minute if there's a reward."

"Put your hands up and toss your kill bag over here!" Parker demanded as he fumbled through his fringe-kissed saddlebags looking for his fringe-free bungee cords to use as handcuffs.

The out-of-work actor swung his bag around like a lasso and let it fly. It slammed against a mausoleum then toppled on to the grass like a pigeon that had ignored its low altitude sensor. Danielle dashed across the pebble-strewn pathway that felt like a corridor of crushed bones to scoop up the bag. "There's nothing in here," she reported as if holding a Halloween sack with no candy in it. "Wait, he had a picnic basket, too." She poked her nose behind his stone throne. "*Voila!* One empty bottle, one half empty, and one with the poison still plugged in it."

Robespierre did a strip tease in slow motion, first removing his babushka, then his wig, and finally his fake fur that looked like recycled roadkill. "Parker, Parker, Parker. What I really wanted was to meet someone who believed in the Bible cover-to-cover, who couldn't be talked out of her faith. Despite your unpretty display of discombobulation, you believe the Bible and live the Bible, unlike your naughty niece, so I am turning myself in to you."

Unglued but not undaunted, Parker pointed his finger at him like a gun. "You're no one to lob accusations at anyone. I was naughty once upon a time, too."

Hawk sat in a heap on top of that heap which was his get-up and confessed: "I'm better off turning myself in here than stateside. Europeans don't like fast food, football, free toilets, or capital punishment. Doing what I wanted enslaved me. The more I did what I liked, the less I liked what I did. I know I can only be liberated by being incarcerated."

"Hedonism is hell on earth, and hell *after* earth," Danielle chimed in.

The Big Bad Wolf tied his babushka around his neck like a polka dot noose. "Sin isn't what it's cracked up to be. It doesn't give you what you want even after you've given it all you've got. Nothing is fun any more. Nothing is anything any more. Farewell, cruel world!"

"Why do you suddenly want the Bible to be true after trying so hard to debunk it?"

"I don't want it to be true, but I know it is. I figured that out after trying so hard to debunk it. Something Seabright said stuck with me. She said she believed the Bible because it told her things she *didn't* want to hear. That means it isn't a product of our imagination."

Parker propped his boot on a headstone. "Wishful thinking theology?"

"*Oui.* Christianity is the most ridiculous religion I've ever studied, with the exception of every other religion. It's obviously not man-made whereas you can see man's fingerprints on every other religion." Hawk swung his fake fur like a matador then bowed as if lowering the curtain on his act. "Substitutionary atonement isn't man-made. It isn't *fair*."

"Love isn't fair," Parker explained as the shadows threatened to silence the light.

She wasn't buying it. "You've cried wolf too many times for me to think you're not one."

"I fear I am one." Hawk dropped on to all fours, growling and howling as if incapable of playing any theatrical part without overacting. "I've indulged my animal impulses so many times that I feel like a veritable *loup-garou.* A werewolf."

"Man is a wolf to man. *Homo lupus homini.* Make sure you put that in your book, Danielle." Parker stepped between his niece and nobody's grandmother as if he were her bodyguard. "Keep your distance, and I'll hear you out," he said, a missionary at heart.

Robespierre fell forward on to his picnic basket, crushing it as if to demonstrate how crushed he felt. "Danielle, I picked up the little Civitas Dei Scripture cards you were placing around the airport when you arrived in Paris. You gave me hope that the Bible was true, so I followed you, but soon you dumped off the entire stack of Scripture cards at a duty-free shop. I knew you were in a state of confusion, so I capitalized on your confusion by testing your faith."

Her mouth popped open like the nose on a cargo plane. "I thought you started following me when you saw me steal that *boules* ball at Parc Chien by the Eiffel Tower."

"No, but that gave me additional ammunition to use against you. If you Christians only knew what sin does to you and to everyone around you, I doubt you would make such a pet out of it. You blow holes in the boat of your own salvation. That you sinned so flagrantly in front of someone who wanted to harm you proved to be a happy coincidence, however."

"I've come to realize there are no coincidences in a Christian's life."

"Then God orchestrated that incident when you started dancing with the devil, or the devil incarnate, my real nickname. That day I saw you at the airport I thought you cared about me, but when I saw the way you lived, I lost all hope. I hated you for my hopelessness. That's when I decided to frame you for as many murders as I could imagine. I *hate* hypocrites."

"Takes one to know one, *Father* Robespierre! You lied to me about the Bible, yourself, and my future, and you just lied to me about sabotaging Parker's bike," she snapped, tempted to inebriate herself with hate. "Look, I need to say this to keep the devil off my back. I'm sorry. I thought I owed it to myself to have a good time and blew it big time. Will you forgive me?"

He covered his eyes with his arm, reeling backwards as if drunk. "You are asking me to forgive *you*?" His eyes grew wide as tires. "This is insane, insane but horridly lovely."

"Excuse my love for things legal," said Parker, "but a number of lawyers who tried hard to disprove the Bible wound up converting to Christianity after examining the evidence."

"Is that so?" Robespierre reached under the liner of his picnic basket. Afraid he was going for a weapon, Parker body checked him backwards into a tomb as if a hockey game had broken out. Laughing like a hyena, the guzzling guru stuck his arms straight up in the air as if some unseen force had placed him under arrest. He then raised his legs to the upright position as if also smitten with mad cow disease.

"I assume this unassuming posture so that you will not feel threatened as we wait for the Paris police."

Danielle dug through the bottom of the basket. "He was reaching for these handcuffs."

"*Oui,* I want you to lock me up, because I can no longer survive the gravity of my depravity. I don't want to do what I want to do any more, so I brought these chains to set me free, to break the vicious cycle I trapped myself in." He howled like a wolf again. "I have no weapon. Strip search me if you must since I will stand butt-naked before God soon enough."

"Spare me the melodramatics," Parker commanded, brandishing an empty bottle like a club. "I'm not going to make the mistake of trusting you like my niece and nephew did."

Robespierre stopped howling and rolled over on his side. Not knowing what to expect, Danielle stepped back a few more paces and brandished a bottle of her own.

The cagey cleric belched into his arm pit. "I could be partying in the Riviera right now without paying an emotional penny for my crimes, so that should prove I'm sincere."

"The police were within days, maybe hours, of capturing you, so you would've paid a pretty penny indeed," Parker replied without belching into either arm pit.

Danielle mumbled in her uncle's ear without taking her eyes off the killer. "I thought the police and the paper said Robespierre had been captured in the Riviera."

"They were wrong. The man pretending to be Robespierre was a con named Jacques Monet. He discarded his phony pony tail and pantaloons after knocking off a petrol depot."

"It's hard to find good help these days," Hawk laughed, demonstrating that he still had extra sensory auditory powers. Drawing his legs into a mawkish fetal position, he whimpered, "Help me?" He then held out both of his wrists like flagpoles.

Not knowing if the howling heretic was setting them up to take them down, Danielle gingerly handed Parker the handcuffs. He pulled open one silver circle and then the other, his hands shaking like an anorexic after an espresso. "The Gospel isn't chained but you will be." He latched the metal jaws around both of his wrists. "It can set you free no matter where you are or who you are, but it won't erase the temporal consequences of your sin."

Danielle called his bluff, "If you are sincere, you can study the Bible in prison and become an ambassador in chains. Paul wrote his best stuff from prison, stuff that became the Bible."

"That is quite the *volte-face*, my voluptuous fiend."

"I'm no fiend now." She noticed the stitches on his wrist. "What's a *volte-face*?"

"An about-face, a reversal. The boat of your beliefs has tipped over."

"No, the Holy Spirit uprighted what you tipped over. As for the Bible that I once hoped was wrong so I could do wrong, I just learned a French phrase that I'll pen in this Bible I'm going to give you: *Honi soi qui mal y pense.* Shame to him who thinks evil of it."

"I hear hope!" He flailed his chains as if reaching through the darkness for something.

"Of course there's hope," said the German American in Paris, drawing courage from a torrent of prayers, "but first you must renounce the devil and all of his works."

Hawk's body contorted into unnatural shapes as if he were enduring a sensational outdoor electrocution. "Satan, I renounce you and all of your demonic power in my life in the name of Jesus Christ, and I command you to take your leave of me!"

Parker braced his legs against a tomb while holding the heretic down in order to prevent him from splitting his skull open on the coffin lid. "Satan, I bind you and all of your evil, unclean spirits and cast you out of this man in the name of Jesus Christ of Nazareth! I plead the blood of Jesus over him and Danielle and me, so go where Jesus sends you!"

Danielle stepped over the wrought iron railing to help Hawk when she realized he was thrashing about the tombstones like a blind man. She placed his kill bag under his neck to soften the blows as he writhed like a snake. Unable to escape the self-imprisonment of his rebellion, the libertine finally gave in to God, but not without a fight. His body bolted off the ground then fell back again as if zapped with electric shock paddles. For a moment, all was quiet, but Parker soon found himself bracing Hawk in a headlock like an alligator wrestler. "Don't loosen your grip!" Robespierre warned them. "Something evil left me, but it might come back again!"

"It won't if you don't let it. Live clean or demons will play house inside the tabernacle of your flesh again," the motorcycle missionary explained. "Read that Bible Danielle gave you."

His face and hands were cut from the action of his own face and hands. "Do Christians still visit people in prison?" he bleated, suddenly embarrassed by his appearance.

"I will."

"Then there's hope. All I wanted is hope." He wiped the drool off his chin. "Why aren't the police here yet? I thought I would be behind bars by now so this nightmare would end."

"You'll make it. We'll help you. There's nothing to be afraid of," Parker reassured him.

"What I'm afraid of, is 'Christians' who don't possess what they profess."

Danielle felt a flush of shame pass over her as if he had opened an oven door. "I've been praying for you, and I'll continue to pray for you. I'll come and visit you too," she added timidly.

"I don't want you to come anywhere near me. You're just the kind of 'Christian' I hate."

"She's not any more," Parker defended her.

"She was the day I came to test her faith. Shakespeare said, 'By my foes, sir, I profit in the knowledge of myself.' Ergo, I hope you will profit by my telling you what you don't want to hear. Every time you acquiesced to one of my temptations *avec plaisir,* Nietzsche's words echoed in my ears: 'His disciples will have to look more saved if I am to believe in their Savior.'"